MAFIO$O

PART ONE

Melodrama Publishing
www.MelodramaPubishing.com

FOLLOW
NISA SANTIAGO

Mafioso - Part One . Copyright © 2017 by Melodrama Publishing. All rights reserved. No part of this book may be used or reproduced in any manner whatsoever without written permission except in the case of brief quotations embodied in critical articles or reviews. For information, address info@melodramabooks.com.

www.melodramapublishing.com

Library of Congress Control Number: 2017909508
ISBN-13: 978-1620780800

First Edition: October 2017

Printed in Canada

BOOKS BY
NISA SANTIAGO

MAFIO$O

PART ONE

NISA
SANTIAGO

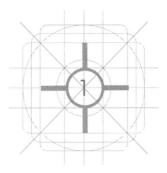

September 1994

The pearl white BMW 535i sailed east on Linden Boulevard, nearing the Cypress Hills projects between Sutter Avenue and Linden. The car was clean and brand new, fresh off the lot from the dealership in Long Island. The air conditioning was on blast, protecting the driver from the intense heat outside, as Mary J. Blige's "Love No Limit" played from the speakers. The sound system was so crisp, Maxine felt like Mary J. was in the back seat singing.

Twenty years old with a lot to look forward to in her life, Maxine was an exquisite woman. She had ebony skin, high cheekbones, and bright eyes framed by long lashes, and her long, luscious black hair came flowing down to her shoulders. Though petite, she was curvy in the right places, and she had a contagious smile. She sported a diamond tennis bracelet, a Rolex watch, and DKNY gear. Her hair was always done, and she always had money in her pockets.

Maxine was in her second year at John Jay College and wanted to be a lawyer, but her one weakness was Scottie—her sexy, thuggish bad boy. Scottie was a fledgling drug dealer making money in Brooklyn. The car was a gift from him.

Upbeat and thinking about her man, she sang loudly to the track, nodding to the beat. She drove past the Cypress Hills projects and continued toward Blake Avenue in East New York, where her parents owned a newly built two-story brick home that came with its own driveway—a luxury in Brooklyn—and was surrounded by a wrought iron fence.

Maxine's parents were hardworking, law-abiding citizens who instilled morals, education, and hard work in her from the time she was young. They tried to keep her separated from the harsh reality of the street life.

From the time she was born, Maxine had a roof over her head, plenty of food to eat, clothes on her back, and two loving parents. Having all that was a rarity in the ghetto, and for a long time, Maxine followed her parents' rules and lived morally.

Until Scottie came into the picture. Scottie took her virginity and spoiled her with expensive gifts. He was becoming her guilty pleasure.

Maxine stopped at the bodega near her home. She had a taste for some gummy bears and a Snapple. She climbed out of her new car looking sporty in a miniskirt, tank top, and white Nikes. All eyes were on her, because of who she belonged to. The men could only watch and admire her from afar, knowing Scottie was nobody to fuck with. He had come out of the Lafayette Gardens projects, and he had a grimy reputation across town.

Maxine strutted into the old bodega with Scottie on her mind. The pearl white 535i sparkled on the dilapidated block. The girls lingering nearby gawked at her, wishing they could have what she had.

Maxine picked up a few things inside the store and placed them on the counter in front of the Puerto Rican clerk. She smiled at him. He smiled back. He rang up her items, and she paid him with a twenty-dollar bill.

Maxine gathered her items and exited. The minute she stepped out of the store, Sandy glared at her, looking like a devious bitch with her protruding belly. Four months pregnant, she was mad at the world.

"Look at dis dumb bitch here!" Sandy shouted, flanked by her two younger sisters, sixteen and seventeen.

They both glared at Maxine too.

Maxine wanted no trouble. Her smile turned into a worried look. Sandy had always been a bully to the weak and was a well-known booster and troublemaker in the hood.

"I don't want any trouble, Sandy," Maxine said humbly.

"What, bitch? You don't want any trouble? Bitch, you *is* trouble." Sandy, her eyes filled with pent-up rage, got in Maxine's face.

"Come on, Sandy. You're pregnant," Maxine said.

"That's right, bitch—pregnant by Scottie—and don't you forget it. *I'm* carrying his baby, not you, bitch."

The news made Maxine grimace. She felt like she'd been kicked in the gut. *How could he? Is it a lie?* Sandy had always had a thing for Scottie, and Scottie was no angel. He was the man every bitch wanted, and most had sampled his dick more than once.

"Wh-what?" Maxine asked, her voice trembling.

"I'm carrying his baby, bitch. What? You thought he loved you? You thought he was gonna be faithful to your ass, bitch? Fuck outta here, you dumb, bird bitch! You think you better than me?" Sandy was so close to Maxine's face, her spit landed on Maxine's lip.

The sisters were inching closer to Maxine too, ready to attack on Sandy's command.

Maxine stood there, timid and afraid. She was no fighter. She couldn't protect herself from Sandy or her two sisters. They were savages—raucous and extremely ghetto. Maxine stood there, hoping she would leave the area unscathed.

The diamond engagement ring on Maxine's left hand caught Sandy's eye. "He bought you that ring?" she asked.

It was too late to hide it from her. Maxine became even more afraid. "I got no beef with you, Sandy."

"Fuck that shit! Yo, he bought you that ring?" Sandy asked again, her voice loud and loaded with jealousy.

"Your beef is with Scottie, not me."

By now, a small crowd had gathered around Sandy and Maxine, many of them hoping to see a fight today.

Maxine just wanted to disappear. *Why did I stop at the store?* She was almost home. Now doom loomed her way. It seemed like there was no escaping a confrontation with Sandy, who'd always been jealous of her.

Sandy had been fucking with Scottie for years, and he had never given her anything. Not even a bite to eat. She did everything for him—hour-long blowjobs anywhere and everywhere, anal sex, fucking his brains out whenever his dick was hard. The only thing Sandy had to show from her sexual escapades with Scottie was the baby in her stomach. Yet, he hadn't claimed it. Sandy didn't want to become just a nagging baby mama to Scottie. She wanted him in her life full time, but it seemed impossible if Maxine was around.

"Yo, you a fuckin' crab bitch, fo' real!" Sandy yelled.

Maxine repeated, "Sandy, I don't have any beef with you."

Thwack!

The slap came out of nowhere. Sandy struck Maxine so hard with her open hand that Maxine's face whipped around. It felt like the right side of her face was about to melt from the sting of the attack.

"Bitch, we got beef now! What?" Sandy scoffed.

Maxine stood there in tears, as the crowd laughed and jeered.

"Ooooh! Yo, she hit that bitch into next week, yo," someone joked.

"Yo, she violated that bitch," another said.

"I'm not trying to fight you, Sandy," a teary-eyed Maxine said. "You're pregnant."

"What, bitch? Pregnant or not, I'll still fuck ya bitch ass up! What? Do somethin'!"

Maxine could only stand there, defeated in shame and fear. She could do nothing. Trepidation swelled inside of her.

"Sandy, please, let me pass. I want to get to my car and go." Just a few feet away was Maxine's white chariot on wheels.

"Fuck that car! I should bust out your fuckin' windows!" Sandy had her fists clenched.

One of Sandy's sisters exclaimed, "Sandy, stop toyin' wit' this bitch and fuck her ass up!"

They crowded around Maxine. It seemed like a fight, or a beat-down was inevitable.

Maxine felt like a bug caught in a spider's web. There was no escape. *Victim* written all over her, her lip quivered.

Sandy didn't care about her pregnancy at that moment. Now, she felt like she wanted nothing to do with Scottie. The only important thing to her now was fighting for her respect. "Yo, watch me do this bitch," Sandy hollered, a fierce look in her eyes.

Maxine knew the attack was coming. She had nowhere to run. She wished her best friend Layla was around.

There was another slap to her face—louder and harder. The tears trickled down Maxine's face.

Sandy taunted her. "Bitch, what? Go ahead, bitch, fuckin' leap! I dare you."

Everyone was anticipating a fight, but then a minor miracle came Maxine's way.

Two uniformed beat cops turned the corner and walked toward the gathered crowd. The cops fixed their eyes on the people standing outside the bodega.

One cop asked, "What's going on here?"

"Ain't shit goin' on, pigs!" a young block-hugger yelled.

"Fuck the po-lice!" another shouted.

Maxine found her moment. She calmly slipped away and walked to her double-parked car. She climbed inside and drove off.

Sandy could only watch as her opportunity to beat Maxine down slipped through her fingers.

Instead of going home, Maxine drove to Lafayette Gardens projects. She was devastated by the news of Scottie getting Sandy pregnant. She couldn't stop crying.

Few people in the hood had cell phones, but Scottie and Maxine did. She dialed his cell phone repeatedly, but he was OT on a drug run and not answering. She left him several messages.

Two weeks before fall, Brooklyn was experiencing a heat wave, and everyone was on the verge of misery. Lafayette Gardens projects was alive with the thugs and drug dealers lingering from block to block, gambling on the corners, and drinking malt liquor. The kids played in the gushing waters of fire hydrants, while the fiends searched to feed their addiction. The area was notorious for violence and drugs. The projects were a breeding ground for violence. One would think the 88th Precinct being directly across the street would impede the criminals, but it didn't. The murders and crime were continuous, like the 88th Precinct didn't exist. Niggas just didn't give a fuck!

Maxine arrived at Lafayette Gardens, marched up the urban pathway leading to the lobby, and made a bee-line to the elevator and pushed for the third floor. She banged on Layla's apartment door with a sense of urgency.

Layla opened the door and saw her friend's disgruntled expression. "Yo, what's up, Maxine? What happened to you?"

"Sandy just came at me."

"What?"

Maxine stepped into the apartment and told her ghetto friend everything that had just transpired.

Layla became animated with rage. She was a lot more upset than Maxine had anticipated.

"See, I told you to stop fuckin' wit that nigga. He ain't no fuckin' good, Maxine. But fuck that shit! We gonna find that bitch an' handle her triflin' ass. I don't like her ass anyway."

Layla readied herself for battle. Her long hair went into a ponytail, and she tied a red scarf around her head. She applied a thin layer of Vaseline on her face to avoid getting scratches and scars, although she wouldn't let Sandy get that close. She reached for her pistol and knife, placed both into a small bag, and quickly got dressed.

By now, Maxine was wavering. She wanted no trouble, and Layla could easily create a world of pain. Layla was a violent beast. A hustler, drug mule, and dealer, she shoplifted and loved to fight. She was a hardcore banger, down to the bone. The two became friends in junior high. Layla loved hanging around Maxine because it was easy to control her, and she became Maxine's guardian angel in the streets.

The two marched out of the building and headed toward the white Beamer. For Maxine, it was too late to turn back. Ready to exact revenge in Maxine's name, Layla was hyped, and there wasn't any calming her down. She lived and breathed for moments like this.

Maxine pulled away from the curb with nervousness. With Layla carrying a pistol and knife in her car, she feared the worst.

"Yo, before we make moves, stop by the store," Layla said. "I gotta get me a Dutch."

Maxine came to a stop at the first bodega she saw. Layla jumped out of the car and went into the store. Maxine left the car idling. She was in deep thought. *I should have just gone home.* Knowing Layla, things were about to get serious.

Two minutes later, Layla came back to the car. She pulled out the Dutch Masters cigar and a whole bag of weed and rolled up while Maxine drove. Maxine was never a regular smoker; occasionally she took a few puffs because Layla was always encouraging her to do so.

It didn't take long to arrive at Maxine's part of town. The sun was gradually setting, but the heat was still lingering. The girls parked in front of Sandy's building on Sutter Avenue. The area was typical Brooklyn, filled with people and traffic, and the dry cleaner and the supermarket across the street had people coming and going. The heat didn't discourage folks from loitering outside. The hustlers drove by in their nice whips blasting the latest rap music.

Biggie Smalls' new album, *Ready to Die,* was the talk of the town. It bumped from passing cars and out of apartment windows. Biggie Smalls was Brooklyn born and on the come-up. Finally, Brooklyn had someone to claim as one of its own. He was making a name for himself in the music industry, and Brooklyn had only love for him.

Layla took a pull from the blunt and simmered in the passenger seat. "I got your back, Maxine. Don't even worry. I'm gonna handle this bitch for you. Real talk."

Maxine was even more nervous now.

"That's her building right there, right?" Layla pointed to the seven-story structure.

Maxine nodded apprehensively.

"You know what floor that bitch is on?"

Maxine nodded. When they approached the apartment and knocked, there was no answer. Either no one was home, or Sandy was ducking them.

"It's good, yo. We got plenty of time. We gonna fuck this bitch up."

The gun on Layla had Maxine worried. She didn't want it to be that kind of party. Layla was unpredictable, and though Maxine considered her a friend, there had been times when Maxine found herself in hot water with her parents because of Layla.

While they waited in the Beamer, Maxine's cell phone rang. It was Scottie finally calling her back.

She was about to answer it, until Layla intervened. "Nah, don't respond to that nigga right now. Fuck him!"

"But I need to talk to him."

"Yo, let that nigga wait. You shouldn't be sweating that nigga; have him sweat you. He out here gettin' the next bitch pregnant, got you lookin' stupid, an' you gonna answer the first time he calls you? Fuck that!"

Maxine let his phone call go to her voice mail.

"That's my girl. Don't let that clown nigga play you for a fool, Maxine."

Scottie called back, and Maxine sent him to voice mail. Layla smiled, seeing her friend finally had the backbone to stand up to the nigga.

For an hour Scottie kept calling, and Maxine ignored his calls. She knew he would be furious. He'd already left several messages on her phone. She knew he hated to wait and to be ignored. If she was in class, he expected her to leave just to take his call.

Maxine went to his voice messages and listened to the first one. She put it on speaker for Layla to hear.

Scottie's rough voice boomed through the phone. "Yo, what the fuck, Maxine? Why you ain't answer the fuckin' phone? You call me wit' some drama shit about some bitch bein' pregnant an' you don't pick up? Pick up the fuckin' phone!"

Maxine deleted the message.

"He should be upset," Layla said, "wit' his cheatin' ass."

Maxine played the second message. Once again, his rugged voice roared through her cell phone: "Yo, you bein' a fuckin' bitch right now, Maxine. You fuckin' hear me? Answer the fuckin' phone, bitch, because you got me upset right now. I swear, I'ma fuck you up, bitch. Where you at? You got me callin' you over and over an' you ignorin' me. When I see you, I'm gonna fuckin' hurt you."

"He ain't gonna do shit. I got your back, Maxine. Don't even sweat that nigga."

Maxine played his third message.

This time he shouted, "That new whip I bought you, I'ma fuck it up an' snatch that shit back, bitch . . . have you walk ya ass around Brooklyn. Take them shines away too, bitch, since you wanna play games wit' a nigga an' not pick up the fuckin' phone. I'ma see you, bitch."

"He ain't your type," Layla said. "Why you love that nigga?"

"I just do," Maxine uttered quietly.

The fourth message he sent differed from the others. "Look, Maxine, forget what I said before. I was just angry wit' you because I feel you let that bitch Sandy get in your head. She's a lying bitch, talkin' 'bout she's pregnant by me. I don't fuck wit' her. But I fuck wit' you, an' I got so much love for you, Maxine. I'm not tryin' to lose you, you feel me, ma? Yo, just call me back so we can talk."

Maxine could hear music in the noisy background. He was in the club. She looked at Layla.

Layla said, "No, don't fuckin' call him back."

Maxine listened to her friend. It was all she did—listen to others.

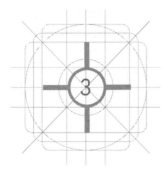

It was nearing two in the morning, and the summer heat had somewhat faded. The girls still sat inside the parked Beamer and waited, stalking Sandy's building. Layla continued to get high. She shared her blunt with Maxine, who reluctantly took a few pulls. The area became sparse with activity and was quiet to some extent. A few dope boys loitered at the other end of the block, playing music, drinking, and shooting dice, their voices echoing in the stillness.

"Yo, where this bitch at?" Layla growled.

"Layla, we should just leave," Maxine suggested.

Layla sucked her teeth. "What? Leave just like that after we been parked out here waitin' for this bitch for hours? I'ma beat her fuckin' ass some more just for havin' me wait this long to beat her fuckin' ass!"

There was no rationalization with Layla; she already had her mind made up to start a fight and get revenge for Maxine. Layla carefully watched every car that passed by and every person entering the projects.

Soon, a Ford Taurus came their way and slowed down nearby. It stopped a few feet behind them. The girls could see a few silhouettes inside the car. They observed a pregnant Sandy, all smiles and laughter, climb out from the back seat. The Taurus drove off, leaving Sandy alone as she walked toward her building.

"C'mon," Layla said.

They both hopped out of the car and approached Sandy from behind.

Layla scowled at the girl. "Yo, bitch, we need to talk."

Sandy spun around, and saw Maxine with Layla. The first thing out of Sandy's mouth was, "Layla, you and I don't got no beef."

"Who done lied to you?" Layla countered with a smirk on her face.

Layla and Sandy were both hood bitches, grimy and 'bout it, 'bout it. They had their reputations, but Layla had a stronger reputation in Brooklyn. She'd shot niggas and stabbed hoes. Sandy knew she was no match for Layla and wanted no parts of her.

Sandy looked at Maxine. Although she had Layla backing her up, Maxine was still a weak, quiet creature. She was too pretty, too decorated with fly things and nice clothing. She wasn't raised for battle on the streets. It puzzled Sandy that Layla befriended such a wack, weak bitch.

"You said you wanted to beat Maxine's ass, so do it, bitch. You about that life, right?" Layla said, instigating things between the two.

Maxine stood next to her friend, looking shocked. She had no intentions of fighting anyone. She only wanted to go home and forget about everything. Why did Layla drag her back into the trouble?

Sandy knew it was a setup. There was no way Layla would stand there and let the ass-whipping go down. The moment she swung on Maxine, Layla would jump into it.

"This isn't about you, Layla. It isn't your beef. It's between me, Scottie, and Maxine," said Sandy, trying to neutralize the situation. "And I'm not tryin' to fight. I'm pregnant."

"You ain't give a fuck 'bout bein' pregnant when you tried to come at my home girl today," Layla countered.

Sandy wasn't a punk bitch, but she had her baby to protect. She never thought Maxine would run and get Layla to fight her battles. Now the tables had turned, and Sandy was the one being bullied, ridiculed, and avoiding confrontation. Sandy felt she should have kept her mouth shut, not confront Maxine the way she did today. But envy had consumed her. Now she wanted to make it to her apartment and lay low, avoid confrontations, and have her baby.

Sandy said, "Look, I'm not tryin' to fight you, Layla. We don't need no beef between us, especially over some nigga. It was a simple misunderstanding between your girl and me, that's all."

"Bitch, you done started somethin', so we gonna fuckin' finish it," Layla spat at her, ready for battle.

Sandy recognized the look in Layla's eyes. It was a familiar gaze of someone dead-set on a fight. Sandy instinctively used one arm to cover her protruding belly, while using the other to reach inside her purse. There was no other way out of the sudden confrontation with a grimy bitch like Layla.

Layla noticed Sandy reaching into her purse. She was about to pounce on her, but to her dismay, Sandy pulled out a pistol and aimed it at them. The .380 was small, but it was deadly in such close proximity.

Maxine was wide-eyed with terror, but Layla stood her ground, angry that Sandy had the audacity to pull out a gun on her.

"You serious, bitch?" Layla uttered, contempt in her tone.

Sandy backed her down with the pistol, shouting, "I told you, don't fuck wit' me. I swear, I'll shoot both y'all bitches, fo' real. You think I'm playin'?"

Sandy slowly backpedaled away from the girls, approaching the building entrance with the gun still trained on Layla and Maxine.

Maxine stood frozen in fear, almost peeing on herself. She'd never had someone point a gun at her. Layla, however, was fuming. She didn't react, though, but stood still and remained cool, knowing Sandy meant every word out her mouth and would shoot them to protect her baby.

"Step the fuck back!" Sandy shouted at them.

Maxine did what she was told, but Layla was hesitant. Then, she finally stepped back as Sandy neared the lobby entrance. With the safe distance between them, Sandy darted inside her building.

"C'mon," Layla shouted.

Maxine didn't want to budge. She had to get her bearings together, but Layla dragged her along anyway. She wasn't going alone.

They ran to the back of the building, zipped into the stairwell in the rear, and raced up the concrete stairs, trying to beat Sandy to her floor and inside her apartment.

Maxine felt it was a dream. No way was she running toward a girl with the gun. Her body was moving, but her mind was telling her to go back. She knew it was a mistake to pursue Sandy, but she followed behind Layla, knowing no good would come from it. They made it to the fifth floor only a few seconds before the elevator chimed.

As Sandy stepped out onto her floor, she met the butt of Layla's gun violently smashing into her face. Sandy collapsed to the floor, dazed from the blow. She desperately tried to defend herself and her baby by swinging wildly at Layla, but she missed.

Layla was all over her, viciously, shouting, "Bitch, you pull a fuckin' gun on me?"

She lodged a hard kick to Sandy's side, followed by another blow to her head from the butt of her gun.

Sandy was down, bleeding heavily and defeated, but Layla wasn't done with her yet.

"Hold this!" Layla said to Maxine, putting the gun in Maxine's hand.

Maxine didn't want it, but Layla, possessed with rage, wanted to teach Sandy a hard lesson about disrespecting her.

Reluctantly, Maxine, scared to death, took the gun.

Layla had felt like a punk when Sandy pulled the gun out on her. She wouldn't tolerate it. She didn't want word to get out that some bitch had pulled a gun out on her and she did nothing about it. Layla reached for Sandy's own gun and thrust the butt of the .380 into her face repeatedly, spewing more blood.

"You pull a gun out on me, bitch?" Layla shouted, smashing the pistol into Sandy's nose and breaking it.

"Layla, you're gonna kill her!" Maxine screamed.

Layla, her mind warped with anger and fury, didn't care about Sandy or her baby. She assaulted her with the gun and her fist.

Maxine was overcome with worry. Despite her dislike for Sandy, she tried to pull Layla off Sandy. Layla temporary turned on her and struck her with the pistol. The gun crashed into her ribs sharply, and Maxine doubled over from the blow, feeling pain shoot through her body like lightning striking her. Maxine clutched her side and fell to her knees. She was sure something was broken inside of her.

It was absolute madness inside the hallway.

Layla continued her assault on Sandy, the floor turning crimson from the attack. She banged Sandy's head against the concrete floor until her eyes closed and she became silent.

Layla finally stopped pistol-whipping and bashing Sandy's head against the ground and released her from her grip. Layla was breathing hard, trying to catch her breath. Pregnant Sandy was brutally beaten, and blood was everywhere on the floor.

Maxine went to aid the girl, hoping Layla hadn't gone too far.

The scuffle and the screaming alerted neighbors. Sandy's grandmother, Carol, opened her apartment door and gazed down the narrow hallway to see her granddaughter lying lifeless on the floor and the girls standing over her. She saw the blood and screamed, "They jumped Sandy! Wake up! They jumped Sandy!" Carol hurried to wake the two sisters.

A shocked Maxine was on her knees cradling the unresponsive Sandy. She had blood on her hands too. She looked up at Layla, who showed no remorse.

Still breathing like she'd run the NYC marathon, Layla looked down at Maxine and uttered the words, "You gotta stay and tell the police it was self-defense. She attacked you. You saw the gun, Maxine. She pulled a gun on you—and you defended yourself."

Maxine heard her talk but didn't understand what she was saying. "What?"

"You got my back, right? She came at you, Maxine. You gotta tell the police what happened."

"No! I can't." Maxine was trembling and scared to death.

"You can. You need to," Layla said, almost like it was an order. "If we both run, then we both get caught. I got too many priors, Maxine. They gonna lock me up forever. You good. You in college, and they ain't gonna crucify you like they gonna do me. I did this for you, Maxine. I had your back. Now you need to have mine."

Maxine nodded. She could hardly think logically. It was all happening too fast. Layla handed her Sandy's gun and took her own back.

Before Layla fled into the stairway, she snatched Sandy's purse—the thief in her couldn't leave it behind. "I love you, girl," were the last words she said to Maxine before fleeing the scene.

Maxine was left with the severely beaten Sandy, who still hadn't moved.

If Maxine thought the night had gone wrong earlier, it was about to get a whole lot worse. Sandy's young sisters came charging out the apartment in T-shirts and panties to aid their sister like race horses being released from the starting gate.

Seeing Sandy lying in a pool of blood enraged them. They attacked, beating up the petrified Maxine until the police came and took control. They arrested Maxine and the sisters, and the paramedics went to work on trying to keep Sandy alive.

Meanwhile, Layla had dashed across Fountain Avenue, as she frantically tried to escape the cops swarming onto the scene. Two cops immediately gave chase through the projects, but she got away.

July 2014

Scott sat at the helm of a large, ornate table in a room that boasted some of the finest furniture ever made and rare artwork painted by eighteenth-century artists. Eight others sat at the table with him: Whistler—his right-hand man; his three lieutenants—Meyer, Bugsy, and Lucky; and four soldiers. Scott wore an expensive, dark-blue, three-piece, two-button suit. He occasionally took a few puffs from a Cuban cigar he held between his fingers and exhaled a thick cloud of smoke around him. A diamond Audemars peeked from underneath Scott's cuffs, and his diamond-encrusted pinky ring shined. He looked into the faces of all eight people, each one dangerous and deserving of a seat at the table. Once a month, he called a meeting to overlook operations. This was grown-man business, and they all were respected in the streets and by the boss man.

His organization was divided into several factions—cocaine, which was run by Meyer; heroin, run by Bugsy; and methamphetamine, which Lucky ran. Scott ran his multi-million dollar organization old school, like his heroes—Al Capone, Meyer Lansky, Lucky Luciano, and Bugsy Siegel. These four men were iconic in his eyes. They'd come from nothing and taken what they wanted in life with force and wit. They'd all become feared, notorious gangsters in their time, and their names forever lived on, like legends.

Meyer and Bugsy were his nineteen-year-old twin sons. Lucky Luciana West was his daughter. She was eighteen and the only female besides her mom to sit at the table among the men. Nobody dared fuck with Lucky, who was witty and cunning and busted her gun just like the men if she needed to. Coming up behind them, Scott had another set of twins, Bonnie and Clyde, who both were fifteen years old, and last, there was nine-year-old Gotti. There was another son, Capone, who was stillborn. No one was allowed to mention his name.

Scott and his wife thought it would be cute to name their children after legendary mobsters. They had never given a thought to how it would appear to society. Every last one of his children was involved in the family's drug dealing business and illegal activity.

Scott's kids were smart and had learned the family business quickly. All three lieutenants reported directly to Whistler, who reported to Scott. Even though they were Scott's kids, there was no break in the rules, so they all followed the chain of command. Scott wanted to keep his kids disciplined. It was the only way for them to learn. Business would never get handled correctly if they ran to Mommy or Daddy every time there was a problem. Scott refused to coddle his kids. If his coke lieutenant felt that the heroin lieutenant was stepping on his toes, then they brought their gripe to Whistler, who would then bring it to Scott's attention, and there would be a sit-down. The three siblings were very competitive, each wanting their activity to net the most money for the family business, and to impress their father. Despite the competitiveness, the siblings still loved each other deeply.

The soldiers who sat at the table were the muscle for the family. Their only job was to kill their enemies and protect the family, product, and the money. If money and drugs had to be transported, the soldiers came in tow, armed with a license to kill. They were there to make sure all went well, and that all was protected. One particular soldier, Luna, was a crazy, callous cowboy with a hair-trigger finger. Thin and dark skinned, he was young, black, and handsome, and he just didn't give a fuck. His eyes were dark like space and told a story of anger and bitterness. Scott was like a father to him, and Luna would die for the family.

The sit-down today was about expansion. Lucky had brought the matter to Whistler's attention, so she could broach the subject with her dad. She had stumbled upon a very lucrative area in Delaware. The addicts were addicted to everything, but their main vices were heroin and meth.

"There's money down there, Dad—lots of it," Lucky said. "We can all eat off this one area."

Scott was listening. He knew all about expansion, having gone from a fledgling Brooklyn drug dealer to a major drug kingpin in twenty years. He did it all—murder, racketeering, extortion, and bribery. In fact, he'd swum in crime and bathed in blood to come up from the gritty streets of Brooklyn to living like a music mogul. Expansion was never a bad idea, but it could be costly in terms of money and lives.

Scott was smart, and he was careful. He'd paid his dues, having done five years in Attica for conspiracy to sell cocaine. While incarcerated, Scott struck up a friendship with Gino, a Mexican goon with ties to the Sinaloa Cartel. When Scott was released from prison, he tracked down Gino, who introduced him to a connection with the cartel. There was something about Scott that Gino liked and trusted. With Gino speaking highly of Scott, the lieutenant from the cartel gave Scott a chance. From there, he assembled his personnel and cut and packaged cocaine and heroin.

A year out of Attica, and Scott was moving thirty kilos of both products in a month, impressing the cartel. To not step on the other main dealers' toes in NYC, Scott created a council, an eight-man organization modeled after La Cosa Nostra's Italian mob families to deal more efficiently with other black and Latino gangsters. The council settled disputes and handled distribution problems.

By 2010, Scott's operation had spread throughout all of New York state and into the Mid-West, Connecticut, and West Virginia. His organization was handling multimillion-dollar loads of heroin, cocaine, and meth in over fifteen states. Scott set up multiple front companies to protect some of his assets. He had numerous car dealerships, a scrap yard, several laundromats and dry cleaners, night clubs, and a strip club. He owned real estate, pawn shops, and was also becoming a developer.

Scott had insulated himself from the streets and the daily drug operation via his children and Whistler. He sat back and enjoyed the fruits of his hard and deadly labor. He felt Elliot-Ness untouchable, but one could never be too careful. Besides keeping a low profile while his net worth was in the hundreds of millions, he was always watching, learning, and keeping tabs on his foes and friends.

"You feel expansion is necessary?" Whistler asked.

"Why not? Delaware is a state that everyone keeps sleeping on, and I'm telling you, we get our grips in certain areas and we can pull in roughly a half a million weekly," Lucky said, "if not more. Shit, niggas hustlin' down there right now are makin'—what—a hundred grand a week off their inferior product right now. And their shit is weak, Dad."

"Good vetting," Scott said.

"I learned from the best," she replied. "You told us, Dad, never get too comfortable in one area, never keep your eggs in one basket, and before you make moves, do your homework, and make sure it's A-plus work."

Scott quizzed, "What else?"

Lucky thought there wasn't more to it. She shrugged.

"I taught you to never build your empire on someone else's land."

Whistler added, "Exactly. Who's runnin' the ship down there now?"

"Some niggas from Baltimore. They call themselves DMC . . . Deuces Money Crew. And the man they report to, his name is Deuce. What they're pushing, the fiends can't even get a good minute high on. It ain't shit, but they're making millions in just this one section alone off that weak shit they got. Dad, we go down there with what we have, the purity in our shit, and we can make money hand over fist. It's gonna be a flood of money."

Scott said, "Expansion into Delaware means getting your hands dirty, baby girl. The takeover. Are you ready for a war with this crew?"

"Dad, you know my blood." Lucky smiled. "Our blood don't pump red Kool-Aid. I'm ready to make this family some more money."

"Unnecessary violence brings the attention of the police, and sometimes the feds, and in a small state like Delaware, the backlash of going to war could be devastating to the family business," Scott said.

"The sweet thing about this area, Dad, is the nearest police station has been corrupted by greed. Deuce got a few of these pigs on his payroll. I know this for a fact."

"Lucky, you should just stick to what you know," Meyer said. "Fuck Delaware! We too big of an organization to be going to war with some clown niggas called DMC over some small patch of grass."

Lucky spat at him, "Did anyone ask you, Meyer?"

"I'm just talkin' here."

"You need to shut the fuck up!" Lucky snapped.

"*L,* I know you ain't trying to rise up and bite at your big bro?"

"Stay in your lane, Meyer, and I'll remain in mine. *Capisce?*"

"You always been ignorant and impatient, reaching for places you know you can't touch. What the fuck is Delaware anyway? Some hick-ass town not even on the map."

"Meyer, I'm so sick of your cynical bullshit! Fuck you!"

"Enough!" Scott barked out at his kids. "This is a family, and we keep any hostility outward, toward everyone else."

Immediately, the minor quarrel with Meyer and Lucky ended. They knew better than to go against Scott.

Scott, his expression blank, took another pull from his cigar as he eyed his children. He loved his kids greatly, but sometimes the nitpicking between them was tiresome. Each had their own potential. They were young, well groomed, and trained for success in the drug world.

Scott didn't need to rush for anyone. He took his time to speak, the room being silent. He took another pull from the cigar and placed it into the vintage ashtray near him.

"Do you feel you can reach out to the officers and strike up some kind of deal with them?" Scott asked.

Lucky smiled and nodded. "Yes."

"I don't want any unnecessary problems in Delaware. This is your thing, okay? So handle it with prudence and acuity."

"Dad, I got this," she assured him.

"I know you do."

Scott listened intently as Lucky laid out all the intel she had gathered about how lucrative a takeover could be for their organization.

With Delaware out the way and Scott sanctioning the expansion, the group continued with other business. Scott turned to Meyer and questioned him about business in the Bronx. Meyer dotted his *i's* and cross his *t's*. He showed his father the books, and the numbers were up. Business was good.

Bugsy was up to bat. Heroin use had increased significantly in the city, with areas like Long Island, Whitestone, and Yonkers tripling usage. The ones who feared needles snorted the stuff up their noses. White kids, especially in Long Island, were hooked on it. It was the 70s all over again.

Tall and handsome, Bugsy wanted to emulate his father. Like Scott, he sat at the table dressed in a sharp black suit, blue tie, five-hundred-dollar shoes, and an Audemars similar to his dad's.

Meyer was the opposite of his twin brother, choosing to sport urban gear, a stylish T-shirt, denim shorts, Timberland boots, a Yankees fitted skewed on top of his soft hair, and a thick gold link chain. He wanted to be the rough and edgy thug in the family. He frequented the strip clubs, showed off his wealth by making it rain on the stage with big bills, and slept around with numerous females. Meyer and his crew could get down and dirty, deadly in the streets, like they had something to prove.

Scott ran a tight ship, and he didn't like to be in the dark about anything. He knew about all his kids' activities—their relationships, their habits, their likes and dislikes, and their wild ways. Out of all his children, Meyer was the craziest. Meyer and Luna were good friends outside the family business, and they hung out together, sometimes got into trouble together, and most likely, killed people together. Scott didn't want his son to get too involved with the soldiers; they did their thing, and his family did their thing. The last thing he needed was one of his kids to get caught up in some bullshit, maybe jailed because of a dumb thing they did. The thought of it always made him cringe. But he couldn't watch over his children and tell them what to do and what not to do forever. They were growing up, becoming their own men and woman.

The meeting was in its second hour. Scott was in no rush for handling business and affairs. If it took all day, he was patient. Each man sitting at the table spoke, either about business or grievances. Occasionally, murders were green-lighted.

Before the meeting ended, Meyer had one complaint he needed to bring up. He looked at his father and said, "Pop, you know that thing we spoke about last month? Well, it's becoming a bigger headache for me."

Scott, chomping down on his cigar once again, stared at his son. He knew the conflict Meyer was talking about was a difficult one.

"This fuckin' cop, he's out of control, Pop. He thinks that badge and gun give him the authority to fuck wit' me. He's getting too greedy," Meyer griped. "Ten thousand a month we pay him; now he wants twenty-five thousand a month. What the fuck is his problem?"

Scott sat in his seat quiet, pondering. Killing a cop was bad for business, but a few rotten apples became too big for their britches. They got greedy and wanted more money for lesser protection. Scott had dealt with these types of officers over the years. Some you could talk to and they would get the message; others were just assholes who wanted to milk a drug dealer dry. But this Sergeant Douglas McAuliffe was becoming a major tumor inside the body. The Irishman was a twenty-five-year veteran of the police force working out of the 43rd Precinct in the South Bronx. He had several killers with badges who were helpful to Scott over the years. But now McAuliffe was looking to retire. He was raising the cost to do business with Meyer and his crew. With his pension, McAuliffe was trying to build a healthy nest egg to fall back on.

But Scott knew the real reason his son wanted the cop dead. McAuliffe had an appetite for black women, which included fucking some of the drug dealers' girlfriends. Word around town was he had a nine-inch dick, and the black women loved to sample his goods. It so happened that Sergeant McAuliffe was having an affair with Lollipop, a popular Bronx stripper that Meyer had become smitten by.

Meyer said, "Pop, he gotta go. He's bad for business, you feel me?"

"We can't just open fire and kill a seasoned sergeant like McAuliffe," Whistler said.

Meyer looked at Whistler. "Why not? It's been done before, right?"

Whistler responded, "Youngblood, you think me and your father are two fools? C'mon, set the record straight—Your issue with this cop isn't just about him wanting fifteen thousand dollars extra a month—He's putting his big dick into the bitch you like."

Lucky chuckled.

"Fuck outta here!" Meyer said loudly.

"Watch your mouth," Whistler sternly warned.

Meyer frowned. "Either way, he's becoming a problem for us!"

Scott gave no answer. Situations like these couldn't be resolved right away, and twenty-five thousand dollars a month was chump change that could be easily recouped in days.

Scott said, "I'll have people look into it."

"Look into it?" Meyer was annoyed with his father's reply.

"What did your dad say?" Whistler chimed at the twin. "You think because you're sweet on some young pussy down at the club that we gonna kill a cop, a sergeant at that, one that is still reliable and resourceful? Think, Youngblood, think—business before your bitch!"

Meyer leaned back in the leather chair and continued to frown.

Scott continued smoking his cigar. Whistler sometimes was his voice; the two connected like brothers. They grew up together and did many crimes together. Without Whistler in his life, Scott knew he would have lost his a long time ago.

Scott sanctioned Whistler, Lucky, and two soldiers to drive down to Wilmington, Delaware to make inroads with cops, dealers, and the fiends. They were to take enough cash to bribe their first cop for information on DMC, and to also get a snitch in the town. They needed to know who the major players in the Deuces Money Crew were, kill them off, and infiltrate the area. They made no move with no intel. Having intel was the key to success or failure.

"This meeting is adjourned," Scott said to everyone.

Right away, everyone lifted themselves up to their feet and left the room.

When the door closed behind the last man leaving, Whistler turned to Scott. "I'm worried about him, Scott."

"He's ambitious, that's all. All my kids are."

"Meyer is sweet on this bitch though. Maybe too sweet."

"Get our peoples on this problem. I wanna know how big an issue this is between the sergeant and my son. Helen of Troy brought an end to an

34

entire city; I don't want this bitch and a cop bringing an end to my son."

Whistler nodded. He embraced Scott with a brotherly hug and exited the room.

Finally alone in the room, Scott walked to the window and stared out at the flatbed truck bringing junk cars into his scrap yard. Covering two acres of land on Stillwell Avenue in Coney Island, it generated legal income for him and helped to get rid of evidence. His scrap yard had proven to be a wise venture.

I t was a stunning six-bedroom estate on ten acres of pristine land in the Florida Keys. The spectacular home was 6,000 square feet of luxury, with nearly every room offering water and garden views. The kitchen boasted granite countertops, stone floors, and high-end wood cabinets, and the master bedroom came with a private balcony and fireplace. Other amenities included a 60-foot boat dock, two golf courses, tennis court, an infinity-edge pool, and an attached mudroom for fishermen. The price tag for such a lavish home was 2.5 million dollars.

Layla sauntered through the grandiose house clutching a tennis racket. She was dressed in a paisley romper over her bikini, wedge heels, diamonds, and pearls. She put a cigarette to her lips and entered the kitchen, where her twin children, Bonnie and Clyde, were at the kitchen island eating breakfast prepared by Gwendolyn, the housekeeper. The twins were beautiful, with cocoa brown complexions, and tall like their father. They were spoiled. They had everything they could ever imagine— clothes, jewelry, sneakers, shoes, and cars, although they had no permit yet. Gwendolyn was preparing a meal of shrimp, cheese grits, and caviar for Layla. It was usually Layla's favorite.

The smell of the food bothered Layla. She said to Gwendolyn, "Throw that shit away. I don't have a taste fo' it right now."

"Late night, Mother?" Bonnie mocked.

"My nights are none of ya damn business, Bonnie," Layla hissed.

"When is Dad coming back?" Bonnie asked.

"Whenever he gets back. You know your father is a busy man."

"Well, we're bored," Bonnie said.

"Then go be bored out of my damn view."

Bonnie sucked her teeth.

Gwendolyn did as she was told and tossed the meal into the trash can. It had taken her almost an hour to prepare.

Layla dropped her ass into the kitchen chair, leaned back, crossed her legs, and said to Gwendolyn, "I need a fuckin' drink. A dry martini—shaken, not stirred."

"Yes, ma'am."

Clyde said, "It's not even noon yet."

"Nigga, do I tell you what to eat or drink?"

Clyde sucked his teeth. "It's your life."

"And I gave you life, nigga," Layla said, "so don't worry 'bout mine." She twirled the tennis racket in her hand. "Besides, I got lessons today, so I need somethin' to relax."

"The next Serena Williams in the house. Whoopee!" Bonnie hollered.

"You little bitch. You keep mockin' me, and I'll throw ya ass in the fuckin' pool and make you stay at the bottom."

"I'm at the pool, Mother. Bye." Bonnie rolled her eyes and sashayed out of the cool kitchen into the heat Florida was known for. Clyde followed behind her.

Though Layla and her husband were filthy rich, owning homes, businesses, and land, she still was a loud, obnoxious, wannabe-bougie bitch. Whatever rich people did, she did. She ate at the finest restaurants in Florida, from South Beach to Palm Beach. She had a golf membership, but couldn't golf. She had lots of money, but no class. The country clubs despised her presence, but they tolerated her and talked about her behind her back. They wouldn't dare say it to her face.

She tried to shed her Brooklyn roots to fit in with the white people down in the Florida Keys. She tried to clean up her speech, but that Brooklyn slang was still in her and would sporadically spill out when she wanted to sound proper. She would say, "Lemme *ax* you somethin'," instead of *ask*. She would behave like this mostly around rich or white folks, but around her family, she gave no fucks.

Gwendolyn brought Layla the martini, and she downed it like a true alcoholic. She smoked another cigarette and gathered the energy she needed to make it through the day. She removed herself from the chair and walked into the living room, where Gotti, her youngest child, was playing his Xbox One. He barely acknowledged his mother while engaged in a session of *Grand Theft Auto*. She went over to him and kissed him on the forehead.

"Ma, you messin' up my game!" he said.

"I just wanted to give my baby boy a kiss. Is that so terrible?"

"You gonna make me die," he griped.

Layla smiled and let him play his game.

Gotti had almost every game for the Xbox. He also had a PlayStation 4 and 3, and so many toys, his room looked like Toys "R" Us.

"I love you," Layla said.

Gotti said nothing back to her, his eyes fixed on the 90-inch flat-screen TV lit up with game activity. The room boomed with reverberation from the surround-sound speakers. He shifted left and right in the seat, his thumbs pressing buttons on the controller as his avatar paraded violently through a computer-generated city, shooting up cops. He was a gamer. He was about to level up.

Layla walked out of the mansion, deactivated the alarm to her pink Maserati parked in the circular driveway, and slid behind the steering wheel. She started the engine, and the car purred smoothly. She turned on the stereo and peeled out of the driveway, tires screeching, like she was in the Indy 500. She merged onto the highway and accelerated to her first destination.

Layla's Maserati entered a large and dusty construction site that was less than two hundred feet away from the ocean. The area was covered with mounds of dirt, bulldozers operating, dump trucks going in and out, an array of building materials everywhere, and over three dozen busy workers. Seven mansion-style homes were being built on the compound, and when finished, would host tennis courts, indoor and outdoor pools, and basketball courts. The main house on the lot would be the largest and would be the parents', and each additional home was for one of their children so they could all remain close. The foundation on each home had already been poured, and Layla would oversee the development occasionally, since her husband was a busy man and always out of town. This was her passion project; from the first shovel dug into the ground, she was there.

She climbed out of her car looking out of place in her romper. Her wedges pressed into the dirt.

Immediately, the site manager approached her in his hard hat and dusty clothes. "Ma'am, you need to put on a hard hat."

Layla shot a look of contempt at him. "And mess up my fuckin' hair? I don't think so. I'm the boss here, so I do what I want."

The site manager sighed, not looking too pleased with her reply.

Layla marched forward. The workers knew who she was. Her presence was a distraction. She was always complaining about something. She was tough, and she took no shit from the contractors who tried to give her inflated bills and high overheads. Layla had to be on her game, knowing these crackers looked at her as a rich, ghetto bitch with no knowledge of their world of construction and development.

"Talk to me, Ron. How are things coming along? We on schedule?" she asked him.

"Copasetic so far," he said, "except for one thing."

"What one thing?"

"The permits for the plumbing are being delayed, and the inspector came by threatening building code violations," he said.

"Delayed? For what reason? And what violations? The damn houses aren't even finished yet."

Ron sighed. "Listen, it's politics, I assume."

Layla frowned. Florida was a hard state to build in. She'd fought for her right to develop something for her family, either with her mouth or her money. She'd come this far, and she would not back down. She gazed around the large site, envisioning something so grand for her family, it would make celebrities envious.

She had a short conversation with Ron before pivoting and marching back to her car. She climbed inside and sped off. Next, it was on to the courts at Wonderlin Tennis in Marathon, Florida, where some of the best played. Layla parked and climbed out of the car with her tennis racket. It was a picturesque day, and she wanted to enjoy it thoroughly. Her tennis instructor, Allison, was one of the best trainers in Florida and charged two hundred dollars a lesson. For Layla, learning how to play tennis was simply something to do.

The Florida Keys had a laid-back vibe, and it was a destination for fishing, boating, and scuba diving. Layla took full advantage of it all. From shopping sprees to tennis lessons, nothing was out of her reach.

Allison was standing on the court in a white tennis skirt, white Nike top, and tennis shoes. She had long blonde hair and tanned skin. She gripped a tennis racket as she waited for Layla. A white woman in her late forties, Allison had lived in Florida all her life. She'd started playing tennis when she was ten years old. By the time she was twenty, she'd already competed in the Australian Open, where she'd won a few matches, and then was defeated in the final of the Open Gaz de France. By thirty, she was burned out, injuring her ankle and losing her edge. From then on, she became an instructor.

Allison frowned at Layla's clothing. A bathing suit and wedged heels was an inappropriate outfit to play tennis in. But Layla didn't care. After her lesson, she planned on relaxing at the beach and guzzling a few more drinks. Layla felt it was her money and her time, so she could do whatever she wanted.

"You look nice," Allison said with a contemptuous gaze.

"I appreciate the compliment. As do you look nice," Layla said, trying to sound like she thought the white lady spoke.

"Let's get started." Allison walked to the opposite end of the tennis court with her racket in one hand and a tennis ball in the other. She bounced the ball, her feet parallel to the baseline. She held the tennis ball with her non-dominant hand and held the racket with her dominant hand. She moved the racket behind her as if to hit with a forehand. Her eyes were on Layla, who looked off balance. She still looked inept as a tennis player after three weeks of training.

"Here we go," Allison said. She was ready to toss the ball into the air and send it flying over the net to the other side. Having served thousands of times, Allison had perfected the art. Her serve could move as fast as a pitch from a major league baseball player.

Layla stood ready on the other side, curved over slightly with the racket in both hands. She eyed Allison, knowing how fast the ball could come to her. Already she regretted not wearing the proper sneakers. Before the first serve came flying her way with the speed of a thrown fastball, she hollered, "Allison, wait a sec!"

Allison paused. "What now?"

"I'm taking these off. I'll play barefoot."

Allison shook her head. Layla was a waste of her time as a student, but she had money. Allison couldn't argue with the steady benjamins the ghetto queen was throwing her way. She was hoping the two-hour lesson went by quickly. The Brooklyn lady didn't belong on her tennis court, but Allison would never say it to her face.

As soon as Layla kicked off her shoes and stood barefoot on the court, she at once regretted it. The sun against the ground was hot, and her pedicured toes felt like they were about to fry on the sidewalk.

"Damn. I ain't know this ground could get so hot," she griped.

Allison sighed. "What size do you wear?" she asked.

"I'm a six."

The tennis instructor huffed. She had tennis sneakers in her locker inside the clubhouse, maybe in Layla's size. It didn't matter if they played or not, Allison was still being paid. As the instructor walked off the tennis court, Layla's cell phone rang.

She hurried over to answer it. She removed the mobile from her purse and looked at the caller ID. Unknown number. Right away she heard a recording saying, "You have a collect call from Louisiana Correctional Institute for Women, do you accept the charges?"

Layla immediately accepted the charges, and the call went through.

Maxine said, "Layla, hey."

"Maxine, hey, did you get the month's commissary I sent you?"

"I did. Thanks, Layla."

"Cool."

"So how's the weather in Brooklyn?" Maxine asked.

"I'm in Florida right now."

"Oh really? What's going on out there?" she asked.

"Nothin' much. Just business."

The two talked like no time had passed, and they were still best friends—like it hadn't been twenty years since Maxine had been incarcerated.

"You good, Maxine? What's the situation wit' them bitches that been fuckin' wit' you?"

42

"I been avoiding them," Maxine replied in a meek tone. "That's all."

"Maxine, you need to stand up for yourself. Damn, fuck a bitch up."

"Layla, I'm no fighter . . . never have been."

"That's always been ya fuckin' problem, girl."

Layla could only imagine what they were doing to her girl inside the prison. She envisioned Maxine being raped and sodomized. She saw her eating out a bitch's pussy late nights by force. She saw her girl washing drawers and being punked and beaten. She even imagined a few male correction officers were getting pussy from her.

"I need another favor, Layla," Maxine said shyly.

Layla knew it was coming. "How much this time?"

"Fifteen thousand dollars."

"That same bitch, Shiniquia?"

"She runs things up in here," Maxine said.

"I can handle her a different way, Maxine," Layla said.

"I can't have that on my conscience, Layla. You know that's not me."

"A'ight, I'll put some money into that bitch's commissary and send a check to her fuckin' family. It's no thang. But I hate to see them take advantage of you like this."

"Thank you," Maxine said. "I'll be okay."

The money was to keep the wolves off Maxine's back and give her some breathing room inside the prison. Maxine was grateful that Layla was paying the extortion money. She didn't have to. But she did.

"Maxine, you know what that jury and that fuckin' prosecutor did to you was fucked up. You don't deserve this."

Maxine replied softly, "It was a long time ago."

"I know, but I think about that night every day," Layla lied.

"I try not to."

"You know, Maxine, it's your fault too for not listening. You could have handled things better that day, you feel me?"

"Yeah, I feel you," she replied halfheartedly.

"I told you let's bounce, but you wanted to see blood that night. You were so in love wit' dude."

"Um, hmm."

Maxine allowed Layla to spew lies and say it was her own fault she'd received a twenty-five-year sentence.

Layla continued, "But I held you down anyway like a fool. Shit, it coulda been both our asses up in that fuckin' prison over some nigga!"

Maxine could hear Layla getting upset. "You're right. I was young and dumb back then. And I'm sorry I put you in such a compromising situation."

"No need to apologize, girl. We're like sisters, and I will always have your back."

Layla went on and on about how she was such a good friend for looking out for Maxine and promising her that the day she got out, she would be taken care of—money, clothes, a house, cars. Whatever she needed, Layla promised it would be there for her.

The conversation soon reverted back to Layla's life. "Guess what?" Layla spoke excitedly.

Maxine was nonchalant. "What?"

"I'm building my family something big. My husband and I bought some land down here in Florida, and we started construction on several homes for us and the kids. Can you believe we're putting almost twenty million into this project? I'm gonna send you some pictures when it's done."

It drove Maxine crazy that Layla never had a conversation with her about marrying Scott. One day, shortly after Maxine was incarcerated, Layla mentioned she had gotten married. And then she was pregnant. It was all a mystery until she began sending photographs, and there he was. Scottie.

"How are the kids?"

"They're doin' fine."

"Good to hear," Maxine replied dryly.

"Next time you call, hopefully, I'll have Gotti wit' me. I'll have him speak to his auntie. I know he would like it."

Maxine could not care less. On her last phone call to Layla, Layla asked Gotti if he wanted to talk to his Auntie Maxine, and he refused. He was a spoiled brat. Bonnie and Clyde also declined to get on the phone and speak to Maxine. They didn't care about her. They'd never met her and gave less than a fuck about her and their mother's war stories from the past.

A beep chimed into Layla's cell phone. It was Scott.

"Maxine, my husband's calling. We'll talk later. Keep ya head up, girl." She hung up quickly and switched over to Scott's call. "Hey, baby."

Maxine frowned as she placed the phone receiver on the hook. The dayroom was filled with female inmates and chitchat, and *Judge Judy* was playing on TV. It was the prisoners' favorite show to watch during the day. Dressed in light blue from her shirt to the pants, she turned, looking deadpan. If Layla could see her today, she wouldn't recognize her. A lot had changed about her. Her cornrows were long and fat, and the look in her eyes was a lot harder than twenty years earlier.

Louisiana Correctional Institute for Women (LCIW) in St. Gabriel was the only female correctional facility in Louisiana. The place had been home to Maxine for two years now. Her arrival created no problems with the other inmates and the locals from the state. Throughout the past two decades, Maxine had been moved a few times due to her violent behavior. Inside the prisons, she was known as Max. There was no more Maxine. The only person who called her Maxine was Layla. Layla thought she was still a gentle, weak person people picked on and took advantage of. Layla had no clue about this side of her, and that was the way Max wanted it.

An inmate attempted to turn the channel, but Max quickly shouted, "Bitch, you turn that fuckin' channel and I'll break your fuckin' arm."

The inmate, who was bigger than Max, bowed down and took a seat quietly in the chair.

Inside the prison, Max was top dog. She had plenty of women who pledged their allegiance to her. Her prison record showed a vicious girl and a tough nut to crack. In her last prison, she broke a girl's nose with a metal chair, putting the bitch in the hospital for three days. Before that, she'd assaulted two girls who stole from her by slashing their faces. Both girls were put into ICU, and criminal charges were brought up on Max but were eventually dropped. Not even correction officers were safe from Maxine's wrath. She'd broken a rookie female officer's wrist when the young girl made the mistake of putting her hand through the slot in the jail door. Max had a profound dislike for the woman, and when the opportunity surfaced, she grabbed the guard's hand and twisted it until it snapped. The female officer cringed from the pain and hollered while Max smirked.

Max was now a forty-year-old O.G. doing time for murder. Inside the prison, she peddled drugs, sanctioned hits, and ran the dayroom.

Back in 1994, it was a hard pill to swallow that Maxine, a meek, pretty law student, could beat a bitch like Sandy to death. It was a cold act to kill a pregnant woman, and that stigma stuck with her.

Her parents were highly disappointed and shocked at the crime she was charged with. For years, they felt she had been railroaded into taking the blame for someone else. They were determined to free their baby girl and clear her name from any wrongdoing, but it didn't work out the way they'd planned.

Once upon a time, Maxine saw herself becoming a successful trial lawyer and, subsequently, a federal judge. But that dream died long ago. Now she was consumed by bitterness.

Max took a seat alone and watched *Judge Judy* for a half-hour in the dayroom, then went back to her cell. She sat on her cot and removed a few pictures from under her bunk. They were pictures of Layla and Scott and the life they'd made together.

Although Max had become hardened in prison, the place didn't turn her out. She refused to become a dyke. She refused to ever give her heart to anyone, male or female. She pleasured herself with her fingers, but it was rare because her main desire was seeking revenge on everyone that did her wrong, primarily Layla.

Shiniquia walked into Maxine's cell and asked, "So she gonna send out the check?"

"Yeah, sometime this week," Max said.

Shiniquia smiled. "Stupid bitch."

"Words right out of my mouth."

Shiniquia sat next to Max. They looked at a few pictures of Layla's glorious life with her money and her family. Contempt was on Max's face. Layla had some audacity, showing off her wonderful life to Maxine, when she was the one who'd murdered Sandy and the unborn baby. Not only did Layla allow Maxine to take the fall and carry the weight, she also married Maxine's man, Scottie, and gave him six kids. Max couldn't put the betrayal into words. It stung so deeply, her blood boiled with rage. No one on earth could get over what had been done to her. Max couldn't cry anymore. She was done crying. She'd accepted her fate a long time ago. She'd become the bitch she should have been twenty years ago.

"I'll call my brother tomorrow and let him know we all good on our end," Shiniquia said. Max nodded, her eyes lingering on Scott's picture. So many years later, he was still handsome and looked more distinguished. The picture she liked the most was Scott seated in a high-back leather chair in some office, clutching a cigar and looking stoic. He was wearing a gray suit with a blue tie, had grown a goatee, and a low Caesar haircut. Twenty years ago, she would have done anything for him. He was the love of her life. He took her virginity, and he was the only person she had ever been with.

She remembered the first time they met. She was so childlike and chaste. She was seventeen and about to graduate from a prestigious private school in Brooklyn. Good Shepherd Catholic Academy groomed some of the best young minds in the borough. Maxine was smart and had wanted to be a lawyer since she was young. She had been accepted to several colleges and had scholarships lined up because she was an A+ student. She'd chosen John Jay because she wanted to stay close to home. Her parents were proud of her. They'd raised a fine, beautiful young girl uncorrupted by the grime of the streets. But all that changed a week before her graduation.

❀❀❀

It was a balmy June, with the sun beaming down on the city. Maxine exited the elevated subway on Rockaway Avenue with her school friends. Dressed in their Catholic school uniforms and carrying their books, they talked happily about the coming graduation day.

Scottie, riding shotgun in a black Benz, spotted the beautiful face from afar. Maxine looked his way but turned suddenly. She was shy. Scottie was smitten by her beauty and told his friend to pull over.

He exited the Benz and approached Maxine and her friends. "Congratulations," Scottie said to the girls clustered in front of the bodega.

He had their attention. He was a tall, handsome young man dressed in expensive jeans, a tank top that accentuated his muscular build and tattoos, and Timberland boots.

"Why you congratulating us?" the mouthy girl in the group asked.

"Because y'all about to graduate, right?"

They looked shocked.

He smiled and said, "The yearbook in y'all hands gave y'all away."

They all looked somewhat embarrassed.

Scottie set his eyes on Maxine. He couldn't turn away. It was apparent to the group of girls who he wanted to chat with.

"And what's your name, beautiful?" he asked Maxine.

Maxine's friend Jennifer spoke for her. "Maxine."

Maxine shot Jennifer a look like, *Why did you tell him my name?*

Jennifer shrugged.

"Since y'all 'bout to graduate, let me buy y'all something," he said. "My treat."

One of the girls said, "Oh, you ballin' like that?"

"I do me," Scottie replied.

Maxine was the only one who looked reluctant, which turned Scottie on more. Something about her was alluring. Maybe it was her shyness; he didn't know. He knew one thing for sure, though. He had to have her.

Scottie treated the girls to Chinese food and sneakers from the local clothing store. Maxine turned down his generous offer. How would she explain brand-new sneakers to her parents? She wasn't working.

He didn't push. He respected her decision.

Looking at Maxine, he said to the girls, "Listen, can I get a moment alone wit' your cute friend here?"

"If she's cool with it," Jennifer said.

Maxine didn't know how to react. The thought of being alone with a handsome thug like Scottie sent her into panic mode.

"I need to get home," she said.

"I'll drive you."

"Girl, we good, and he fly. Do you, Maxine. Have some fun for once," Jennifer said.

Maxine sighed heavily. Peer pressure made her accept the ride home. She nervously climbed into the back seat of the Benz, while Scottie sat in front with the driver. Scottie asked questions, and she gave him one or two-word answers, simply smiling and nodding. He complimented her beauty countless times, which made her blush.

It took a lot for her to open up to him. But Scottie was relentless, and she opened up finally. He couldn't drop her off directly in front of her parents' home. She couldn't be seen climbing out of a drug dealer's car. Scottie had his friend park a block away from the house and made his friend step out of the car while he and Maxine stayed seated and talked for almost an hour. He loved everything about her. She took down his number and promised to call him.

A week after Maxine's graduation, Scottie took her shopping. It was her graduation gift. Whatever she desired, he spent cash on. She couldn't bring her new goodies to her parents' house, since it would raise speculation. Scottie suggested she keep her new things at his apartment, and she did. When she visited him, she would change clothes, enjoy his company, and leave for the summer internship her father had arranged at a law office in the city. After work, she would visit Scottie.

At the end of summer of '92, a month shy of her eighteenth birthday, he finally took her virginity. Maxine felt ready. Scottie had always made her feel wanted and comfortable. Whenever he'd tried to force sex, Maxine felt tempted but resisted. Scottie didn't pout; he was patient with her nervousness to have sex.

Meanwhile, Scottie was secretly screwing several other girls in Brooklyn, including Sandy.

The night she lost her virginity to him, it was in his dim bedroom in the project apartment. Scottie gently laid Maxine on her back in his bed. He reached for her panties and slowly pulled them off, exposing her pussy never touched or penetrated by any man. He was excited to be her first. He removed his boxers, put on a condom, then positioned himself between her spread legs.

There still was a tinge of apprehension, but this time she would go through with it. She wanted to show him how much she loved him.

As he slowly penetrated her, she squirmed underneath him. Scottie wanted to take his time with her. Inch by inch, he pushed his erection inside of her, hearing her grunt and moan from her first sensation of penetration. It took a moment for him to get a rhythm going inside of her, but once he did, he was on cloud nine. He was thrilled to transform his girlfriend into a woman. She made him come so hard and strong, his body soared into the stratosphere.

Maxine went from nervousness to ecstasy in less than half an hour. She enjoyed him fully too, and he was all she wanted in her life. For her, there was no other than Scottie. She saw herself marrying him and them having a lovely family together. Just like her parents.

Max sighed internally. She had stared at the picture of Scott long enough. The memories from her past were too painful. She tossed the picture aside and continued to seethe.

"You gonna get your revenge, Max," Shiniquia said. "My brother ain't no joke, feel me?"

Max nodded.

"Yo, that bitch is crazy to think y'all still cool after all these years and after what she did to you. I woulda had my brother do her dirty for free."

Max wanted to execute justice. There was no one else speaking to her. It had been a long time, and she felt forgotten. Everything had changed. No children were coming to visit her, no friends, no family. Her parents were old now, and Louisiana was too far to visit from New York. She only had herself and her reputation to keep her company. The only true friends she'd ever known were the inmates she had been locked up with.

Shiniquia was always good company. She and Max had a lot in common. She was from a rough neighborhood in DC and grew up poor. She had little family, besides her mama, brother, and two cousins. She had no kids, and was mostly a loner. She was thirty-eight and, like Max, was doing twenty-five to life for felony murder.

While high on crack, Shiniquia and an accomplice robbed an elderly neighbor lady who lived alone. It was believed that she kept all her cash and valuables under her mattress. They broke in through the back door of the woman's home after nine a.m., Shiniquia carrying a loaded .22.

They moved quickly. Assuming the woman was at church, they rummaged through the place and tore the bedroom apart looking for cash and jewelry. They were desperate to find something to pawn for crack. Shiniquia turned over the mattress to find nothing. Her accomplice worked the second bedroom.

Suddenly, the woman arrived home and startled them. Shiniquia fired two shots into the old woman's chest, killing her instantly. It was a knee-jerk reaction from someone not in her right mind. Both girls fled but were caught a week later and indicted. They both pled guilty to murder.

Over the past two years, Max and Shiniquia became good friends. Shiniquia developed an attraction for Max, but Max made it clear to all the inmates that she didn't swing that way.

"I trust your brother," Max said.

"He needs the money, and he'll get it done."

Layla didn't know it yet, but she would bankroll her own demise. The fifteen-thousand-dollar check was to go to Wacka, Shiniquia's wild, crazy brother. Wacka was a cruel and disturbed man, and for fifteen grand, he would wipe out an entire family. For now, he would start with the youngest and work his way north.

Max had no regret. The wheels had been set in motion, and there would be no stopping it. She wanted Layla to feel tremendous pain, and Max only saw that happening by attacking the things she loved most—her family and her husband. Twenty years had neither buried Maxine's pain nor dulled her hatred for the bitch who betrayed her. In fact, twenty years inside had only fed the bitterness and intensified her thirst for revenge.

Lucky drove her black Benz G-Wagon down the New Jersey Turnpike. Traffic was flowing freely, and she did 75 mph while Whistler rode shotgun. An inconspicuous white Sonata carrying two armed goons, Tommy and Urge, followed behind them on the Turnpike. Delaware was twenty miles away.

Whistler and Lucky rode in silence for the moment. Whistler was never much for conversation. He had a hard face and a harder stare. Dressed in a neat black suit, he looked more like a businessman than a stone-cold killer and a drug lord's right-hand man. He always looked blank and was an introvert most times. He looked out the window, watching cars pass by, and already he was thinking a hundred moves ahead of the game.

"You think my father trusts me on this move?" Lucky asked him.

"If he didn't, then he wouldn't have sanctioned it."

"I just want to make him proud of me, Whistler."

"He's already proud of you."

"And what about you?" she asked him. "What do you think?"

He stared out the windshield. "You're doing fine."

"I just feel Delaware is the place to make some serious money. I did my homework on these niggas, and they're stupid sloppy. We can annex these muthafuckas like the blink of an eye."

"You shouldn't have gone to Delaware by yourself, Lucky. It was a dangerous move. I'm just happy that your father didn't find out about your recklessness."

"I'm not a little girl anymore, Whistler. I'm a grown-ass woman, and I know how to handle myself. I can travel somewhere and not create attention. Besides, I was carrying."

"I don't doubt that, but always have precaution in this business. You never know. And having a gun on you doesn't always mean security."

"I got *you*, right?" she said, smiling at him. "*You're* my precaution."

Whistler remained stoic—no response.

"You need to lighten up more, Whistler. You always so dry and unemotional."

"Lucky, in this game, one can't afford to have emotions. Emotions will get you killed."

"Whatever!"

Lucky was just like her mother Layla—domineering with a strong personality. Sometimes she could be stubborn, and she got what she wanted by any means necessary. She loved to be in control and took no shit from anyone.

It was a beautiful July day with temperatures in the nineties, and the AC was on full blast in the car. Lucky felt she was too beautiful to be sweating. She had a Beyoncé CD playing in the car, listening to "Formation." Since Whistler wasn't much of a talker, she needed something to engage her.

Eager to start things in Delaware, she sped on the Turnpike. This was her project—her territory. Just thinking about the control she could have over the area made her salivate. They crossed over the Delaware Memorial Bridge, paid the toll, entered Delaware, and shortly arrived in Wilmington. Lucky steered her G-Wagon into the hapless-looking blue-collar town.

Whistler took it all in. The city moved with life, but it wasn't a major metropolis. Every ten blocks they traveled, he noticed a police car. Some areas looked run-down, and some areas were re-developed, but overall, it was still a poor town.

Lucky stopped her truck on N. Church Street and moved near the curb. She kept the engine idling as she climbed out of the truck and stepped foot onto the city ground. Whistler followed her exit, and the goons in the Sonata did the same thing.

Lucky looked around at the people and the properties, and she smiled. Dressed in a navy blue jumpsuit, multi-colored bangles decorating her wrist, and heels, she looked more like a famous supermodel than the daughter of a drug lord. Her long, black hair blew in the passing breeze, and her eyes were covered with large, dark shades.

"You know what I smell, Whistler?" she said.

"What?"

"Opportunity."

Whistler said nothing back. He was there to protect and guide her. Knowing she could be hellfire sometimes, he was prepared to do his job and make sure Scott's little princess was unharmed.

Tommy and Urge stood near Lucky and Whistler with dark, serious expressions. It was easy to tell they were muscle for the two. Standing firm and dressed in black despite the summer heat, each man had a Glock pistol holstered beneath his light jacket.

"We need to move on," Whistler advised. He didn't want to attract too much attention. It was easy to tell they were new in town.

Lucky nodded, and they climbed back into their vehicles and drove off. Soon, the group checked into a DoubleTree hotel on the outskirts of town. Tommy and Urge shared a room on the second floor, and Whistler and Lucky had their own rooms on the third floor.

Whistler removed his expensive suit from his body and carefully placed it on the bed, next to the two 9mm pistols he was carrying. He was a clean-shaven man with a bald head and intense eyes. He was rather meticulous, always well dressed and careful with his things and his movement. He stood in a pair of boxers, his dark skin showing signs of years in the drug game, the streets, and prison. Scars ran down to his abdomen, a sign of his gunshot wound years earlier. There was an old stab wound to his upper back, and another gunshot wound on the right side of his chest. His physique was still muscular and showed little decline, though he was forty-one.

He went into the bathroom and took a needed piss. Afterward, he looked at his image in the mirror for a beat. The stories he could tell. The things he'd seen, and the murders he'd committed—some were personal, but many murders were for business, precaution, and under orders.

Not many people knew Whistler's story—where he came from, who he was. It was a mystery to everyone. Whistler was Scott's confidant, bodyguard, and second-in-command in the drug dealing operation. Still, Scott didn't know everything about his trusted right-hand, although they'd grown up together. Whistler had no children, no living parents, and his quiet demeanor sometimes intimidated people.

A knock at the door disrupted Whistler from his thoughts. He spun around, marched out the bathroom, and retrieved one of his pistols from the bed. He glanced through the peephole and saw Lucky standing outside the hotel door. He loosened up a little and opened the door. Lucky charged into the room excitedly and threw her arms around Whistler and slammed her lips against his. He wrapped his arms around her, and they kissed passionately for a moment.

She took a break from kissing his lips. "I want you, baby."

Whistler closed the door. The last thing he needed was prying eyes. Lucky stood in front of him looking enticing. "You couldn't wait?" he said.

"No, I couldn't. Shit, I wanted to suck your dick on the ride down here." She touched his naked chest, aching to feel all of him inside of her.

They moved farther into his room.

Lucky kissed him zealously once more and felt every bit of her womanhood become moist with anticipation. Her hand reached into the slit of his boxers, and she grabbed his big dick and stroked him into a full erection. She dropped to her knees and wrapped her lips around his hard flesh.

Whistler groaned from the tantalizing feeling of her full lips sliding back and forth around him. What she was doing to him was forbidden in the eyes of her family. Daddy's little girl was sucking a grown man's dick—a man old enough to be her father and there to protect and guide her while in Delaware.

Lucky moaned while having Whistler inside her mouth. She enjoyed pleasing him. She enjoyed feeling the pulsation of his penis inside her mouth and alongside her tongue. Lucky made the forty-one-year-old so weak in the knees he needed to sit down while she continued her blowjob.

Her parents had no clue about their love affair, which had been going on for two years, when Lucky was sixteen years old and Whistler was thirty-nine. If discovered, it would be the end of Whistler. His body parts would be scattered across the tri-state area. Whistler loved her and saw nothing unethical about it, but he was wise enough to keep things between them a secret.

With Whistler's help, Lucky peeled off her clothing and stood butt naked in front of him. Her young body was a marvel to see. Her tits were perky, her mound was shaven, and she had an ass like a bubble.

Whistler removed his boxers and situated himself between her open thighs and thrust inside of her roughly. This was exactly how she liked it. Lucky didn't have time for weak and gentle sex; she loved having her hair pulled, her pussy ravaged, and her ass smacked. Whistler had proven to her repeatedly that he was her guy. He had the stamina of a young bull.

Both of them were rocked by intense orgasms. Lucky, held in the arms of her older lover, always felt wanted by him, and the sex with him never let her down. With their pleasure completed, it was time for business.

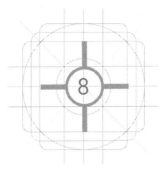

8

Leaving Lucky's G-Wagon parked at the hotel, the foursome climbed into the Sonata and drove into Wilmington. Dust had settled in the urban environment, but the heat still raved on. This time, Lucky was dressed for street business, wearing tight jeans that highlighted her best qualities, a T-shirt, Prada sneakers, and a baseball cap. She sat in the back seat with Whistler, while Urge drove and Tommy rode shotgun.

They turned into a drug infested area via Chestnut Street and stopped in front of the High Low Street Bar, a hole-in-the-wall cornered on Chestnut and Dunkin Streets. Word around town was that fiends and a few dealers frequented the bar, the owner once a heavy drug user himself. The plan was simple—gather information by cash or force. Whistler felt that paying off fiends for information could be useful, since drug users were the ghetto internet of the neighborhoods. They knew the players, the users, the locations, and who did what.

Tommy and Urge stepped out of the car and walked into the bar. The two men could be as subtle as a lion in a bank. Whistler followed them into the place. Inside was seedy and dim, with sketchy characters scattered everywhere. The place was smoky with a low ceiling, and its ripened wood furniture looked ready to come apart at any moment. It was happy hour, with one-dollar beers and three-dollar drinks from seven to ten p.m. The jukebox played Otis Redding's "Let Me Come on Home." The chitchat was thin, but the feel of the place was tense.

Whistler approached the bar. He stood out immediately in his black suit, gold Rolex, and alligator shoes. His two henchmen took a seat at a corner table, where they remained quiet and alert.

Whistler told the bartender, "A shot of whiskey."

The man nodded and went to fix his drink.

Whistler scanned the place and noticed everyone and everything. He wasn't worried about the customers that bordered him. Most looked unassuming and listless, and too consumed by alcoholism to become a problem for him.

The bartender set the whiskey on the bar counter in front of Whistler, who passed him a twenty-dollar bill and told him to keep the change. The man was grateful. Whistler downed the shot and asked for another. Two would be his limit.

Whistler pulled out two hundred-dollar bills and slipped them to the bartender, saying, "In fact, drinks are on me right now."

The announcement of free alcohol quickly brought life to the dead inside. Twelve patrons in all felt like they were the luckiest people on earth. Whistler watched them drink everything, from white and brown liquor to Bud Lights and Coronas.

Fifteen minutes went by before Whistler decided it was time to get down to business. He got up from the bar counter and approached his first fool, a lean man with thinning hair, sunken eyes, and dressed in hand-me-down clothing. Everything about him screamed, "drug fiend."

Whistler sat opposite of the man and stared at him intently. "Can we talk, my friend?"

"It-it's your world, friend," the man stammered.

Whistler nodded. "How can I get in contact with the group DMC?"

"DMC? Dem boys are rough," the tipsy one said.

"I just need a name."

"Um, um, maybe Marty," the man said.

"Where can I find this Marty?"

The man shook his head. "Don't know."

After a minute of conversation with him, Whistler thought he was unreliable, figuring Marty was a figment of his imagination. He worked the next patron. His idea was to get the men drinking, because alcohol usually made lips loose, and plus, he didn't want them to hardly remember him and that he was at the bar questioning them about the drug crew.

His next fool was a younger fiend, late twenties with bad skin and bad hair, but he still appeared to be in his right mind. Whistler approached and sat next to him coolly. The fiend locked eyes with Whistler.

Whistler said, "DMC . . . what do you know about them?"

"You got cash on you?" the fiend asked.

The attitude was typical. Free drinks, and these people still wanted more. Whistler wasn't bothered by the bribe; he had enough money to go around. He handed him a twenty-dollar bill.

The man secured the cash in his fist like it was his own soul. He said to Whistler, "Dey from B-more. Nasty group of niggas if you ask me. I don't fuck wit' them."

"I need a name."

"Look for a nigga named Marty. He fucks wit' them grimy niggas."

It was the second time Whistler had heard the name. He felt like he was getting somewhere. He nodded, satisfied with the recent information, as he removed himself from the chair.

The fiend, his hand out, asked, "Can I get another twenty?"

"Where is Marty?"

"Don't know."

Whistler gave him the twenty and said, "We never had this talk, you understand? I was never here."

The fiend nodded. Forty dollars richer, he was ready to disappear from the bar and search for his drug dealer.

Whistler continued to work the crowd. Within a half-hour, he had what he needed. Marty, a man in his mid-twenties, could sometimes be found at an abandoned warehouse near the Christina River. The area was a breeding ground for addicts, prostitutes, and drug dealers.

The foursome traveled to the area and continued their search for Marty. They grilled the fiends and the prostitutes moving up and down E. Front Street, a block littered with abandoned buildings and Christina Park, a central hub for transgressions. At dusk, the area became the devil's playground, with drug users and prostitutes turning tricks in cars or in the park.

Whistler climbed out of the Sonata and stood on the sidewalk, not worried about trouble coming his way. Sometimes he felt he was the devil himself, ready to burn anything in his path. He examined his surroundings with a keen eye, determined to find this Marty character. What were his vices?

He looked at his thugs still seated inside the car and said, "I'm gonna travel on foot. Y'all drive off."

"Why?" Lucky asked.

"Trust me," he responded.

There was no resistance. The car drove off, leaving Whistler in the middle of enemy territory and armed with his 9mm. He figured four people in a car would look off and intimidating to the people. It was best to be alone, ask questions, spread some money, and find Marty from there.

He crossed the street and approached a working girl with long, stringy hair. She was thin, wore a short skirt and halter top, old high heels, and too much red lipstick.

The lady stared at Whistler and smiled. "You lookin' fo' a date, handsome?"

Knowing action speaks louder than words, he teased her with a hundred-dollar bill, and the C-note caught her attention. She charged not even half that for sucking dick and fucking—forty dollars at the most. A hundred dollars was platinum to her.

"What ya want?"

"Information," he said.

She looked confused.

"Where's Marty?"

She shrugged. "I don't know."

"I think you do," he said. "Think harder."

She stared at the hundred-dollar bill in Whistler's hand. It would be a shame for her to lose so much money. She scratched at her arm and fidgeted in her old heels. She looked around her, almost appearing paranoid out of the blue.

"You need to hurry before I talk to someone else," he said, growing impatient.

"Okay, he's at the Enterprise."

"The Enterprise? Where is this place?"

"A block away." She pointed east. "Can I have my money now?"

Whistler was no fool. He said, "Take me there. If he's there, you'll have your payday."

She marched toward the location, and Whistler, alert and observant, followed right behind her. His demeanor dared someone to try him. He passed dealers and fiends and walked the troubled area with no incident.

The Enterprise was a dilapidated, abandoned two-story building littered with drug paraphernalia and rubbish where many fiends went to get high. Whistler followed behind the woman into the darkened area, which reeked of excrement. Stoic to it all, Whistler moved deeper into the structure, casting his eyes on the lost souls that lounged around on the ground. Some fiends who were too weak to stand or move used the columns for support, but everyone appeared to be in a deep trance from whatever drug they were on.

Whistler's alligator shoes trampled against the hundreds of crack vials, crack pipes, needles, and whatnot littered everywhere.

The hooker pointed to a man seated in a folding chair, in the corner of the place.

Whistler stared at him. He was tall and slim with nappy hair. He had some cash in his hand and was dressed in shorts, a T-shirt, and sneakers. Whistler deduced that Marty was a user and a dealer—an odd marriage. He gave the prostitute the hundred-dollar bill, and she left to chase her next high, leaving Whistler to approach Marty. Seconds later, Whistler called Urge and gave him the address.

In exchange for money, and observing that he was in a no-win situation surrounded by Whistler and his two scowling goons, Marty relented and talked. He told them everything they needed to know about DMC's operation.

"They been 'round here fo' two years. The main dude is Deuce. He's a scary muthafucka that nobody fucks wit," Marty explained. "His right-hand man is Jimmy . . . smart and mean."

Lucky asked, "Who's his supplier?"

"Don't know."

"What about his muscle?" Whistler asked.

"Jo-Jo and McCall—they his two top enforcers, an' they ain't no joke, man. Word on the street is, they can skin a nigga alive," Marty said with trepidation. "And there's Rock, Deuce's main dealer in this city. But above all dem niggas is Detective Jones. Don't nothin' in this town move or take place wit'out him knowin' 'bout it. He's the main cop on Deuce's payroll. You get wit' Detective Jones if you need to know anything more."

Whistler and Lucky were pleased with the information Marty had, so they kept their promise, and provided him with some cash.

Whistler let Marty go free, saying, "You mention any word about us to Deuce or anyone, and I'll guarantee they'll find your head in the fuckin' park."

Marty hurried from them, fearing the worst.

"We should've just killed him," Lucky said.

Whistler responded, "His death might raise suspicion."

"I don't trust him," she said.

"I trust his fear."

"I don't. Who you think he fears more, Deuce or us? He don't know us at all, and there's no telling what he might tell those niggas. You should never trust a fuckin' drug addict. They're only loyal to their addiction," Lucky proclaimed.

Lucky was itching to find Marty again and silence him for good measure. This was her project, and she wanted nothing to go wrong. Her goal was to make tons of money for the organization, become a boss bitch, and please her father. She couldn't and wouldn't allow any failures. But Whistler still felt he'd made the right choice.

They exited the rundown row house and climbed into the car. It was getting late, so they went back to the hotel for some sleep and planning. The following day they would search for Detective Jones.

H old him down! Hold him the fuck down!" a male's voice boomed to two men struggling with a single man inside the dark kitchen of an empty restaurant.

The victim was a chubby, young African American man of average height named Nate. He was desperately trying to fight off his attackers. In the scuffle with the two dark individuals, he caught a glimpse of their cop badges. Fearing his own death, Nate tried to reach for their holstered guns, but the two plainclothes cops quickly overpowered him and slammed him against the chopping table. They threw a few shots into Nate's side and into his ribs, causing him to cry out and wince in pain.

"We told you, muthafucka, don't fuckin' run from us!" the taller cop screamed.

They continued punching him in the face, cracking ribs with their brass knuckles, and smashing his head against the table.

Bloody and dazed, Nate stammered, "D-don't kill me." His breathing was sparse, and his body ached from the attack.

The owner of the voice instructing the officers finally loomed from the shadows, and Nate stared at the detective with absolute fear on his face.

Detective Jones said, "Nate, you like fuckin' with us, huh? You think I'm stupid?"

"I didn't do anything," Nate said.

Detective Jones, evil in his eyes, approached. "You steal from us, huh?"

"I didn't, I swear. I'm not crazy enough to take anything from DMC."

"Why you lie, nigga? Huh? You know, I respect a nigga more when he admits to his wrongdoing than for him to open his filthy fuckin' mouth to spew a lie to me when we all know the truth," Detective Jones proclaimed.

"Please . . . Deuce know I'm good peoples," Nate pleaded.

"You see, when you steal from Deuce, you take from me too, you ignorant nigga. You have the audacity to take food out of my kids' mouth, take away nice things away from the wife, and have my family go hungry?"

"C'mon, man, you eaten an' livin' lovely, Jones."

"That ain't the point, muthafucka! It's the principle!"

Detective Jones, his badge and holstered Glock showing, stood menacingly in front of Nate. He was a tall and brutish man, standing a muscular six one with a narrow face and intense eyes. He had black skin and cropped hair with a five o'clock shadow. Detective Jones was a ruggedly handsome man with a penchant for power and control. He moved with confidence like he owned the place. Being a city detective, he was cocky and arrogant, acting like he ran the entire police force.

"Stretch out his fuckin' arm," Jones instructed the subordinate cops.

They did what they were told, forcing Nate's right arm onto the chopping table. He resisted, but they held him down firmly and exposed his entire arm for Detective Jones.

"You see, Nate, your action comes with consequences. I mean, it's how the world works, right? You do something stupid, like steal from Deuce *and* me, and the penalty for that is pain, maybe death. Depends on my mood." Detective Jones chuckled.

"C'mon, Detective, not like this. I got kids, man."

"Yeah, and so do I and every swinging dick in this damn state. You feel exempt from the consequences because of your bastard kids?"

The metal meat tenderizer was the perfect tool for the detective to use. It was meant for cooks, but tonight, it would be used for torture and pain.

Jones gripped the weapon. "I'd be lying if I told you that I didn't enjoy this part, because I love it."

Detective Jones went to work on Nate's right hand, hammering away at his knuckles and fingers.

Agony shot through Nate immediately as he cried out in excruciating pain.

Detective Jones hammered away several more times until Nate's hand looked like chopped meat. The hand turned crimson, and every bone in it had been broken.

Finally, they released Nate, and he fell to his knees in tears and in pain, clutching his bloody, contorted extremity.

Detective Jones stood over the suffering man and smirked. "Be grateful that I didn't take your fuckin' life."

Nate whimpered.

Detective Jones final words to him were, "A thousand dollars paid to us within forty-eight hours, or I'll take the hand next time, or your life. Depends on my mood."

Detective Jones and his men left the kitchen, leaving Nate to grovel in his pain and suffering. They departed from the restaurant through the rear entry and stepped into an alley where Jones' burgundy Cadillac Escalade was parked.

Detective Jones lit a cigarette. It felt good hurting somebody, to relay a message violently the way he did. He said to his men, "I bet fifty dollars that he doesn't pay in two days."

Plainclothes officer Andrew laughed. "You just wanna take our money too."

"Hey, making money is always fun," Jones replied.

"Well, I like my money where it is right now—in my pockets," Andrew said.

The trio had been corrupt cops for many years and created a bond of trust between them. Collectively, they'd made hundreds of thousands of dollars for themselves and for DMC. Also on Detective Jones' payroll were several uniformed cops. They did it all—drug dealing, extortion, bribery, protection, security, providing inside information to DMC, and occasionally, murder.

The cops shared a quick laugh in the alley and then climbed into their vehicles, Jones in his Escalade and the plainclothes detectives in the unmarked squad car, and went their separate ways.

Before going home, Jones had a few more stops to make. He collected from two more drug dealers that owed money to DMC, and his last stop was at a whorehouse, a DMC establishment under their protection. Detective Jones went to collect dues from the place and received a complimentary blowjob from one working girl there.

While seated in his truck, he counted the day's take from the dealers and the whorehouse and came up with fifteen thousand dollars, much of which was his. He smiled. Life was good. He felt untouchable because he was collecting so much money from DMC.

The following morning, Detective Jones arrived to work at the police station on N. Walnut Street. At roll call, he joked with his fellow officers until their sergeant took the mic.

The sergeant expressed his concern to the officers about the growing drug problem in their city. The night before there were four overdoses and two shootings, leaving one dead.

Detective Jones frowned at the fatal shooting. He was unaware of the death and planned to find out who killed someone in his district without him knowing about it.

"Y'all ladies are dismissed. Be safe out there," the sergeant said to his troops.

As hordes of cops left the room, Detective Jones lingered behind. On the sly, without prying eyes, he slipped the sergeant an envelope filled with cash and whispered to him, "It's been a great week."

The sergeant quickly took the payment and concealed it on his person.

"Who's the stiff in the shooting?" Jones asked him.

"Some stupid local dealer that stepped on the wrong toes. Nothing to worry about," the sergeant said. "He took one to the head. No suspects so far. It wasn't you, right?"

"No," Jones quickly answered.

"Okay, cool. This arrangement with Deuce is cool as long as we keep the violence and murders low."

"Everything's copasetic out there."

The sergeant was appeased.

"I got runs to make," Jones said.

"Stay safe."

Detective Jones walked out of the police station and got into an unmarked black four-door Dodge Charger to patrol his city. Jones was everywhere in Wilmington. There wasn't a drug dealer he didn't know about or a situation he wasn't connected to. If it weren't for the badge, then he would be a bad guy—a dealer and enforcer himself for DMC. He shook down dealers, collected money, held court with major players in discreet locations, and subtly harmed the people who got out of line or didn't know how to play ball with DMC.

It had been a long day, and Whistler took notes of everything, watching the detective work his charm on the streets in his black Charger. Whistler was very familiar with men like him. The badge meant nothing to them; they wanted to be cowboys and hide under the insignia of law enforcement. Dealing with Detective Jones would be nothing new in Whistler's world.

Lucky and Whistler followed Detective Jones from his workplace to his beautiful home in Westover Hills, where he lived with his wife of ten years and his three kids—ages ten, seven, and two. Westover Hills was an affluent area a few miles from the city, where the tree-lined streets were broad and quiet.

Detective Jones owned one of the best houses on the block. The price for his five-bedroom beauty was half a million dollars, which he couldn't afford on a cop's salary. He parked his police vehicle in the large driveway and got out.

Whistler and Lucky sat patiently and discreetly for two hours outside the detective's home. While seated in the car, they talked about their future together. Lucky was deeply in love with Whistler, and he felt the same about her. But their love could never be displayed publicly. It would be a death sentence for Whistler and a downgrading for Lucky. There never was going to be a right time to tell the family, since he'd defiled Scott's little girl.

"I love you, Whistler," Lucky proclaimed wholeheartedly.

"I love you too."

They kept it professional inside the car—no kissing, no holding hands, and no public display of affection.

Finally, Detective Jones made his departure from the home. He was dressed differently, with a black T-shirt under a light jacket, jeans, and Nike Jordan's. He looked like he was ready to attend a ball game, and he was still flashy with his big-face diamond watch and Cuban link diamond chain. He climbed into his Escalade and drove away.

Whistler, determined to have a few words with Jones, followed him to a bar on 4th Street in a sketchy part of town. The place was popular and busy and a known DMC location. Detective Jones entered the bar like he owned the place. He greeted a few people, and the respect was evident.

Lucky and Whistler went inside, but it was hard for Lucky to remain low-key in a black hip-hugging dress and six-inch heels. The boys inside stared hard at the young temptress. Whistler remained nonchalant and readied for anything.

It was risky to contact the detective in hostile territory, but this was their only chance. Whistler and Lucky took an empty seat in the back, keeping a keen eye on the detective as he met with Katrice, a beautiful, curvy woman. The two kissed, and Jones smacked Katrice on the ass playfully. She giggled. They downed a few drinks and mingled.

A half-hour passed, and like always, Detective Jones was the life of the party. He continued to fondle and kiss his mistress openly. He was a killer and a drug dealer with a badge, and yet, everyone appeared to love him and treat him like he was their golden boy.

"We gonna do this or what?" Lucky asked, ready to make her move.

Whistler nodded.

Lucky stood up and strutted toward the bar. Turning down a few male advances, she kept her eyes on the detective and subtly stood near him.

Being the dog he was, Detective Jones couldn't help taking in Lucky's sexy dress, and his eyes immediately filled with lust. She was too beautiful to resist flirting with. With Katrice away in the bathroom, he turned her way and said, "Can I buy you a drink, beautiful?"

"I'm fine," Lucky said.

"You're new here. Where you from?"

Lucky smiled at him and slyly slipped him a small folded piece of paper. He looked hesitant to take it, but he did. She then said to him, "How about I'll buy you a drink?" She walked off, leaving Jones baffled.

Detective Jones unfolded the piece of paper and read:

We can make you a richer and more powerful man than Deuce. If you're interested in hearing about our offer, meet me in twenty minutes at this location. We come with gifts.

The detective turned to look for Lucky, but it was like she had vanished into thin air.

The address wasn't far from the bar, ten minutes to be exact. He frowned, not knowing what to think of it. It could be a setup, but he needed to investigate it. The cop in him made him go.

After Katrice came back from the bathroom, Detective Jones cut their date short, downed a shot of tequila, and left the bar in a hurry, leaving her scratching her head. He hopped into his truck and sped off.

Immediately, Jones got on his cell phone and made a call to one of his subordinates. "We might have a situation. I need you to meet me at this location right away."

As he hurried across town, he checked his 9mm for ammunition and his backup holstered at his ankle. He was ready for any confrontation or a trap. The detective stopped his truck in front of the row house and killed the ignition. He cautiously scanned his surroundings as he climbed out of the vehicle.

His backup, Detective Phelps, arrived just in time. "Jones, what's going on?"

"I don't know yet, but I'm gonna find out."

Right on cue, Lucky emerged from the row house.

Jones no longer looked at her like a good piece of pussy to fuck, but as a suspect. He narrowed his eyes at her and barked, "What games you playin' with me, bitch? You know who I am?"

Lucky smiled. "I do. That's why we came to you."

Whistler soon flanked her, and in good faith, tossed a small duffel bag at the detective's feet.

"What's this?" Jones asked.

"Our gift to you," Whistler said.

Detective Jones looked at Phelps, who shrugged. He was just as clueless. Both men seemed on edge. Jones crouched toward the bag and slowly unzipped it. He was shocked to see what was inside—bundles of cash, totaling fifty thousand dollars. It was a lot of money.

"Now that we've gotten your attention, can we talk?" Lucky said coolly.

Jones was still apprehensive, but he followed them into the row house, with Phelps having his back.

"Only you, Jones," Whistler said. "Your partner stays outside."

Jones shot back, "He goes where I go."

"Our deal is only with you, not him," Whistler said sternly.

Apprehensive and reluctant, Jones yielded to Whistler's demands and told Phelps, "I'll be okay."

Phelps nodded.

Detective Jones followed the duo into the kitchen. He still clutched the bag of money.

Lucky lit a cigarette and looked at the cop. "You're impressive. I like you a lot. You're very flashy on a cop's salary—nice home, nice truck, nice watch. Nice side-bitch too."

"Who are you people? And what do you want with me?" Jones spewed irately.

"Look, we know everything about you, Detective Jones," Lucky said. "You're connected to Deuce and his crew. You're everything to them. Now we want you to become everything to us."

Jones chuckled faintly.

"As you can see, we mean business," Lucky said, pointing to the bag of money he held onto.

"And why should I trust you two? I don't know shit about you or him."

"You know my father, detective?" Lucky asked.

"Who the fuck is your father?"

"Scott West. From New York."

Jones had heard the name and some of the stories.

"What would he want with a small city like Wilmington, Delaware?" Jones was bewildered by the proposal.

"The same reason Deuce is down here—there's lots of money to be made in Delaware, and we want in. DMC's product is far inferior to ours, Detective, believe me. With what we're bringing to the table, profits will increase tremendously."

"And so will the violence and bloodshed. We got a good thing going here, and why would I want to rock the boat, huh?"

"Either with or without you, we're coming, Detective, and we're gonna be like Rome, annexing everything we can get our hands on. When it's over, there will be nothing left to profit from," Lucky said.

Jones suddenly found himself in a tight spot.

"Right now, all we're asking from you is intel," she added.

Detective Jones stood silently for a beat. He had a lot to ponder quickly. "I want double what DMC was paying me."

Lucky nodded.

"I can assure your crew, your dealers, your drug mules, and enforcers absolute protection from my people when they're in town from New York. You'll have complete run of the town to profit anywhere. You're gonna have to murder DMC's crew within a reasonable timeframe, because Deuce will know a new product has infiltrated his town, and he will know I'm cooperating with his competition. But no violence—no bloodshed in my city, you understand? I can't have bodies dropping and piling up all over the streets. This isn't New York—that type of heat in Wilmington will attract attention and the feds. And I can't protect you from the feds."

Lucky smirked at his comment. Like *he* could protect *her* from anything.

"We have our ways of doing things, Detective," Whistler replied coolly.

If they had to dump the bodies in another town over, burn, or bury them, it would get done.

Jones told them if the money was right, he would give up everything he had on Deuce and the DMC. Just like that, the cop switched sides. The deal was made, and Jones shook hands with Lucky and Whistler.

As Jones was about to leave, he said, "Don't underestimate Deuce. He's as vicious and as deadly as they come. You deal with him, or he'll deal with you."

Lucky took the warning in stride.

Outside, Phelps asked Jones, "What was all that about?"

Jones chuckled slightly. "We just got traded to the other team."

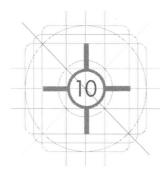

D ressed in a black tank top highlighting his lean physique, black cargo shorts, and black Nikes, Meyer took a pull from the Newport as he watched Lollipop work the stage at She Dreams. He sported a huge diamond in his left ear, diamond rings, a Rolex watch littered with small diamonds, and a long chain around his neck. He was too jumbled with diamonds. Having been born into street royalty, Meyer felt he was the prince of Brooklyn and the Bronx. She Dreams was his personal playground and a front business for his father. He was young, rich, handsome, and powerful. And spoiled. As promiscuous as he was flashy, he'd had sexual relations with several of the strippers.

"Diced Pineapples" blared throughout the Bronx strip club. The provocative song made all the girls amped.

Wearing nothing but clear stilettos and glitter, Lollipop put on a show for the audience. She twerked and spread her legs, exposing her sweetest asset. Then she moved to the pole and worked it like a snake, coiling around the polished staff and suspending herself a few feet above the stage.

Lollipop was flexible and beautiful. She had bouncy tits, a flat stomach, and a brown bubble-ass. Her hair was cropped and wavy, bringing out a cute baby face and innocent smile that could light up the dim club. She slowly worked her way down to the stage and rolled around on the parquet, showing off her tricks for a treat.

Meyer stood there amused and stimulated by the sight of Lollipop and her talents. Jealousy bubbled inside him as he watched customers touch her naked assets and tip her money.

Out of all the girls he'd fucked in the club, she was the only one who made him feel a certain way. He didn't know why. She was twenty years old, and a high school dropout with a one-year-old daughter to support. He took another pull from the Newport and exhaled.

Though young, Meyer was sharp with business and the streets. He learned from the best, and he came from the best. His father trusted him with handling a multi-million-dollar segment of the family organization.

Meyer controlled the cutting, packaging, and sale of cocaine in the city, operating two large mills in Brooklyn. Both locations were fortified with walls reinforced with steel and concrete, high-end surveillance equipment, and guards with machine guns. He supplied the dealers in the urban jungles of New York City. He was their connect.

One of Meyer's goons whispered something in his ear.

Meyer nodded, finished his cigarette, and flicked it away, not caring who it hit. He pivoted and marched toward his office in the back of the club. Upon opening the door, he saw Sergeant McAuliffe seated behind his desk, looking like he owned the place. The cop had company—one of his corrupt pigs to have his back.

Meyer frowned at the presence of the sergeant. "Why you here?"

"It's that time of the month, Meyer. Come on, don't act brand-new to this," McAuliffe replied.

Sergeant McAuliffe was in his early fifties and was as white as they came. He was a big-framed man with a thick chest and a large stomach, a long, wide face, a head full of salt-and-pepper hair, and the puffy eyes of a drinker. He wore a wrinkly shirt with no necktie, blue jeans, and discount footwear.

"You in my seat," Meyer complained.

"It's a very comfortable chair; I might have to get me one myself."

"I'll give the chair away to charity, since you done tainted it. Maybe you can take it to your cage to rot in," Meyer mocked.

Sergeant McAuliffe smiled. "I don't want to do a song and dance with you, Meyer. I'm a very busy man. And, lately, you've been shaky with me. Now, the new arrangement I proposed—did you run it by your father?"

"I have."

"And?"

"I'm still waiting for an answer. To jump from ten grand to twenty-five grand a month—it's a significant number."

"Spare me the pity. Your family can afford it."

"How about we replace you altogether?" Meyer said, half-joking.

"Is that a threat?"

"You can take it as you want, Officer—I never liked you in the first place," Meyer said through clenched teeth.

Sergeant McAuliffe lifted himself from the expensive leather chair, looking at Meyer coolly. His partner remained nonchalant in the corner. McAuliffe removed his badge from his hip and placed it on the desk, for Meyer to see.

"You wanna measure dicks, you smug little muthafucka? I guarantee mine will have a longer reach. I've been loyal to your family's organization for years. Helped protect y'all from prosecution and demise, so don't fuck with me! You see that badge? You know what that is? That's longevity, muthafucka. You may think you and your family are untouchable, but I've seen your kind come and go. Your family has some staying power because your father has always been smart. He understands there's a balance to this thing we do. You start tipping the scales, and everything will fall over. Don't a damn thing last forever—You better not forget that."

Meyer stood silent. He was unmoved by the cop's speech. He nodded to his only goon in the room, who promptly disappeared.

McAuliffe picked up his badge from the desk and reattached it to his hip. "I'm retiring soon, and I want to be very well compensated for all I've done for this organization. Twenty-five thousand dollars a month isn't asking much. And don't think I haven't been keeping records. I'm not ignorant. Y'all have a file on me, and I have one on y'all. We can throw all the dirt and get muddy, but what's the point? Balance is the way of life, right?"

Meyer's thug returned and placed a large stack of cash on the desk. Meyer locked eyes with McAuliffe. "There's your payment—ten thousand. Like I said before, the raise hasn't been approved by my father yet. We'll see."

Sergeant McAuliffe picked up his money and smirked at Meyer. "This doesn't have to be difficult, Meyer."

"It doesn't have to be anything," Meyer replied.

There was substantial tension between the two men. Meyer had his personal reason for not liking McAuliffe. The sergeant's penchant for young, black pussy had become a nuisance to him. He was an asshole and a pervert.

Before departing, McAuliffe grinned at Meyer. "You have a very balanced life, Meyer." He and his secondary left the room.

Meyer stood in the doorway and kept his eyes trained on McAuliffe as he moved through the strip club and then stopped where Lollipop was standing. He gently took her arm and pulled her closer to him, whispering something into her ear that produced a smile and a giggle from her. Then he fondled her ass.

Seeing this, Meyer fumed, ready to storm the officer's way and confront him with violence. But his henchmen took hold of his forearm and prevented him from moving further.

"Meyer, not now," one of them said. "Keep cool. He's tryin' to fuck wit' you."

Sergeant McAuliffe knew how Meyer felt about Lollipop. He purposely looked Meyer's way to see the reaction from him. The officer smirked then exited.

Meyer couldn't help himself. He went to Lollipop. "What the fuck did he say to you?"

She saw the seriousness on his face. "He said, 'Smile, because you're too beautiful not to.'"

The thought of that white pig touching Lollipop enraged Meyer. "Meet me in my office," he ordered her.

She went into his office, and the moment she stepped foot through the door, Meyer roughly slammed her against the wall and wrapped his hand around her neck. "I don't want you talkin' to that muthafucka, you hear me?"

"He came to me," she said.

"I don't give a fuck! You stay away from him, you hear me?"

Lollipop nodded meekly.

Irritated by the cops' presence, Meyer needed a release. He ripped away her thin G-string, pushed her against his desk, and turned her around forcefully. She knew the deal. Her body curved over his desk, he quickly unfastened his jeans and took her from the back, slamming himself inside her. Lollipop was *his* bitch, and he wanted no one else touching her.

11

Scott rode with Meyer and Bugsy through the Holland Tunnel heading toward New Jersey. Also with the family were three armed goons. The roomy, luxurious black Lincoln Navigator provided enough space for everyone. The trip to New Jersey was mostly quiet, each man occupied by his own thoughts. Scott puffed on a cigar and gazed out the window. He was seated beside Meyer, and Bugsy rode shotgun.

Bugsy looked casual in a pair of black slacks, a button-down, and shoes—wanting to emulate his father—and Meyer looked hood in a throwback Falcons jersey, jeans, beige Timberlands, and lots of jewelry.

Finally, Scott broke the silence inside the vehicle and said to Meyer, "I want you to pay Sergeant McAuliffe the twenty-five thousand a month."

Meyer looked stunned by his father's decision. "You serious?"

"I am."

"But, Pop—"

"It's my decision, Meyer. Don't go against me," Scott advised his son.

Meyer couldn't help but to tighten up his face and look away from his father. He was disappointed. A regular cop extorting them for more money? In his eyes, it showed a sign of weakness. They were an influential family, and McAuliffe was nothing to them. He was itching to get rid of McAuliffe—give him an early retirement party of his own. He remained quiet, longing to change his father's mind.

The Lincoln Navigator drove into a suburban community in East

Brunswick, New Jersey and toward a semi-large church with a large brick steeple pointing into the blue sky. The boys were stunned to be at a church.

The driver killed the ignition, and Scott and his sons climbed out of the truck. They were there to meet their supplier, Javier Jesus Garcia.

"Hell of a location," Meyer joked.

Scott didn't reply to his son's comment. He coolly fastened the buttons to his suit jacket and walked toward the front entrance. His sons and his goons followed behind.

Inside the foyer of the church, the men were greeted by several of Javier's security guards. The men weren't strangers to each other. Javier's men searched the group, and they were allowed to enter farther to meet Javier inside the congregation area.

Javier walked down the aisle, his eyes focused on Scott and his two sons. "You're a punctual man, Scott. One of the things I like about you."

"I don't do CP time," Scott replied.

The two shook hands. There was a level of respect between the two.

Javier Garcia was Mexican-born and raised in a small town of Imala, Sinaloa. He grew up destitute. His life of crime started at eight years old, when he joined a band of thieves to rob and steal from tourists and local businesses. By the age of twelve, he'd graduated from petty theft to drugs, smuggling, and murder. By seventeen, Javier was a seasoned criminal with a fierce reputation and had become a top enforcer, moving up the ranks of the cartel through sheer violence and cunning.

Javier was short with salt-and-pepper hair, deep-set eyes, and a square cleft chin. He was well put-together in his expensive suit and nice watch. He didn't drink or smoke or put any pollution into his body. In fact, he was a vegan who worked out daily and was a healthy man with smooth skin for his age. He was an avid reader, fluent in Spanish, English, and Russian, which was good for business, since he was a supplier for the Russian mafia. He was permanently sharp and focused, and he rarely made appearances. He only met with his top buyers once or twice a year, so they could feel his presence and his power.

A few months earlier, Javier's biggest competitor, El Chapo, had been apprehended by the authorities, leaving the market wide open for more lucrative accounts. Javier Jesus Garcia felt he was more powerful and influential than the president of the United States.

"Come. We talk in the pastor's office," Javier said to Scott.

Scott followed behind Javier into the pastor's office, while Meyer, Bugsy, and the goons on both sides waited in another room.

Scott needed to first make sure Javier had no ties to Delaware or DMC before he infiltrated the area, and second, he wanted to rework a delivery route should Javier green-light the situation.

Out of respect for Javier, Scott chose not to burn one of his cigars, knowing how much Javier hated the smoke around him. The two men sat across from each other in gray Bentwood armchairs.

Javier leaned back and crossed his legs. His deep-set eyes stared at Scott. His look could be intimidating. Though he appeared to be a humble man, Javier was one of the most dangerous, wealthy, and powerful men on earth.

"I'm looking into making a move into Delaware, and I wanted to run it by you first. I wanted to ensure my peoples weren't stepping on any toes belonging to your organization," Scott said.

"Delaware? I have no ties down there," Javier informed him. "You're free to do whatever."

"Good."

With that out the way, Scott went on to his next order of business. Javier guaranteed his product to New York, where his organization had a lot of buyers, and the return on investment was worth the risk.

"It's about the route," Scott said. He wanted Javier's delivery crew to go south from New Jersey to Delaware instead of north to New York.

"And why would I want to change my route?" Javier asked.

"It will be an added risk of moving kilos from New York to Delaware. I figured since you're so close—"

"And I should take on the risk?"

"We should come to a mutual agreement," Scott said.

"If mutual is beneficial to me and my business."

The Turnpike and alternate routes were always dangerous to their organization. State troopers were trying to crack down on drug mules with state-of-the-art surveillance equipment and drug sniffing dogs. It cost money, men, and time to continuously try and outsmart the police and remain covert, and that was why drug organizations could charge more per kilo to drug dealers.

"What is the return on this Delaware move?" Javier asked him.

"From the numbers I've run, roughly a five hundred percent return."

"Impressive. Who would think that such a small state can carry such a high reward?"

Scott smiled.

"I'm afraid that I'm going to have to decline your request," Javier said civilly. "The routes will stay the same. This Delaware situation is too new for me, and their infrastructure is thin at best, nonexistent at worst. My men will continue shipment to New York, and the pickups at the New York City docks will remain. And you will ship the package to Delaware through your men."

Javier was sure about the docks in the city and trusted nowhere else. He had paid protection there with the NYPD and Coast Guard.

Scott was sad to hear the decline. It meant heavier loads traveling via the Turnpike, and more headache for him and his organization. He wanted to share the risk, since he was Javier's New York connection. It would have been easier for the kilos to come to Delaware straight from neighboring New Jersey.

With the expansion into another state, Scott and Javier discussed a new cost per kilo of cocaine and heroin, since Javier supplied both demons. It was the one thing Scott felt they were in agreement on.

Javier stood up from his seat. "I have another affair to attend to, Scott. It's been a pleasure to meet with you, and congratulations on your expansion." Javier extended his right hand, and they shook on their mutual understanding.

Javier left the room while Scott remained standing there. He was still irritated, but he knew not to cross a man like Javier Garcia. He was feared everywhere.

Finally, Scott left the office and reconnected with his sons and goons. He didn't look too happy, and Bugsy picked up on his father's mood. They left the church and headed back to New York.

The ride back to the city was quiet once more, until Bugsy asked, "How'd the meeting with Javier go?"

"I don't need to discuss that with you."

Bugsy didn't push it.

Scott was worth over two hundred million dollars. He came from the rough streets of Brooklyn and made himself into a dominant figure in the underworld by building a powerful empire. Not many men from his era could say they'd done the same. But his accomplishment was only a drop in the bucket compared to what Javier had built for himself. Javier was worth billions. He was international. Scott was somewhat envious, and it irked him that he had to ask permission to move on territory. He'd made a promise to himself that he wouldn't leave the game alone until he made a billion dollars, or he would die trying. He had always been competitive. He always wanted more. And taking over Delaware was another step toward his billion.

Going through the Holland Tunnel, Scott said to his sons, "I ran the numbers for Delaware, and they're respectable."

Meyer asked, "So what you tellin' us, Pop?"

"I want you, Bugsy, and Lucky to temporarily move down there, set up shop, and make it happen."

Meyer frowned, entirely against the idea. "Are you serious? You want us to live in Delaware? What about what we got goin' on here? You want us to just leave it unattended?"

"Your mother and I can handle things in New York. Y'all will be in Delaware."

"Why you doin' this to us, Pop? What the fuck we do?" Meyer continued to gripe. "I got a life here!"

Though Bugsy was reluctant about the move too, he allowed his brother to do all the complaining.

Scott swiftly placed his hand on the back of Meyer's neck, pushing him forward with force. "What I say?" His grip on the back of Meyer's neck was firm. "Until I tell you otherwise, Delaware will be your place of residence. Now shut the fuck up!" He released his clutch from around his son's neck and sat back. He placed a cigar into his mouth and lit it, needing the smoke.

Meyer scowled, massaging the back of his neck. He was fuming, but he remained quiet.

Scott had a few more things to say to Meyer and Bugsy. "Whistler will travel back and forth between both locations. And I will send you some top enforcers for any trouble y'all might have. But I want that city under our organization. I don't care how it gets done, I just want it done. You two understand me?"

"We do," Bugsy answered.

Scott glared at his rebellious son. "Do you understand?"

"Yeah, I know, Pop," Meyer replied.

September 1994

With her right eye blackened and swollen, her bottom lip cut and inflamed, and dried blood on her face, Maxine sobbed in the interrogation room. Sandy's sisters had beaten her severely, and the cops' arrival was all that had prevented the sisters from killing her.

The room was cold, windowless, and bleak. Handcuffed to the metal table, Maxine felt the urge to pee on herself. She had never been in this much trouble before. She had never even been arrested. Now she was in a heap of shit—held at the local precinct for 24 hours before they formally charged her.

The good news was that Sandy was still alive. The bad news was that she was brain-dead, and it was up to her family to pull the plug or not. The horrible news for Maxine was the baby Sandy was carrying had died, which added a murder charge to the indictment. The cops rained down on Maxine with threats of murder and jail time. They wanted her to talk.

"Who is your accomplice? Who was the girl running from the building? Tell us something, Maxine, or you'll go down for this by your damn self," the detective said.

"You're looking at first-degree murder, Maxine. Talk! Tell us something to help yourself!"

"I don't know anything," Maxine cried out.

They drilled her for over two hours, and all they got from her was tears, regret, and apologies. Maxine was in a damaged state. She couldn't believe this was happening to her. She felt alone and so damn scared. Her law education went out the window—she didn't even ask for a lawyer. She wanted to see her parents, and she asked for them repeatedly. The detective told her that they'd been notified of her arrest and were on their way to see her.

"Why did you attack the girl?" another detective asked.

Maxine's eyes were flooded with tears, and her face was stained with panic and regret. She trembled in the police presence, not knowing what to say. They would charge her with murder for the baby's death, and if Sandy didn't make it, it would be another count of murder with a list of other charges. The cops told her she could get the death penalty.

Maxine couldn't envision herself on death row. She was hoping it was a nightmare she could wake up from. But no matter how often she pinched herself, she found herself seated in the hard metal chair and facing a life-changing moment.

"Your parents are here," a detective said, entering the interrogation room.

There was a small bit of relief for Maxine. She couldn't wait to see them. She wondered if her father could perform a miracle and free her from her predicament.

The moment her parents stepped foot into the room, her eyes burst open like a collapsed dam. The sight of her folks brought on complete solemn remorse and guilt. They'd spent their entire lives trying to bring her up right and educated. They would've done anything for her, and now she had let them down.

Her mother hurried to her baby girl and hugged her tightly. Her father too. Because of the handcuffs, Maxine couldn't hug them back. She didn't want them to let go, terrified she would never see them again.

Her father couldn't hold his frustration and anger in. "It was that girl you like to hang around with. What's her damn name?" He quickly belted out, "Layla got you into this mess, didn't she?"

Maxine cried more and didn't answer her daddy.

"Tell us something, Maxine," her mother cried out.

"I'm sorry, Momma," Maxine sobbed.

Her mother held her. "They're going to charge you with murder, Maxine! Murder!"

"Tell them what you know, Maxine. Tell them it was Layla. I hated that girl since the day you brought her around," her father shouted. "I knew she was trouble from day one. Just make things easier for yourself, Maxie—Tell the truth."

The detectives watched the meeting from a separate room. The room was under surveillance. They were hoping Maxine's parents could convince her to save herself.

Maxine's father couldn't hold back his tears either. He wanted his little girl to come home with them.

Maxine didn't say the name everyone wanted to hear. Why didn't she give up Layla? It was because of her Maxine was in this predicament. Layla had taken the situation with Sandy too far. She was still in shock. Maxine had watched Layla beat a woman to death with her bare hands.

She thought about Scottie. She needed him right now.

September 1994

Shocked by the news of the attack on Sandy, Scottie raced back to Brooklyn and arrived home at nine that night. Maxine had been in jail for several hours. He was worried about her and Sandy, who was carrying his baby. *How did things get this far?* Scottie couldn't see the situation coming. Maxine was too passive to beat Sandy down the way the streets were describing it. He knew Layla had to have a hand in the assault. It had her signature written all over it.

Once in Brooklyn, he went to Cypress Hills projects with his cousin and a spare key to Maxine's car. He removed the BMW from the block. An expensive car like that stood out, and he didn't want anything to happen to it. He parked the car in his cousin's driveway. The last thing he needed was a gun charge, so he gave his cousin his gun to hold for him. Then he showered and changed clothes, readying himself to drive to the precinct to see his girl.

Dressed in his Boss jeans and Jordans, Scottie stepped into the precinct looking nonthreatening and law-abiding. He approached the front desk and said to the sergeant, "I'm lookin' for my girl. Her name is Maxine Henderson. Is she here?"

"Your name?" the sergeant asked.

Scottie gave him his name. He didn't know what to expect, but he knew he had to be there for Maxine. He felt guilty about the nasty messages he'd left her. He didn't even know if she was still being detained in the precinct, or if they'd taken her down to Central Booking for processing.

He was met by a detective in the waiting area.

The police heard several theories from Sandy's family about why she was attacked. Scottie's name came up each time. They felt he was juggling two girlfriends at once, playing with their hearts. Sandy was carrying Scott's baby, while Maxine was his main squeeze.

Before Scottie could see Maxine, a detective needed a few words with him. "If you want your girlfriend to ever see freedom again, she needs to say something and implicate the other assailant."

The cops had already run Layla's name, and it was messy. She had numerous arrests for grand larceny, petty larceny, assault, drug dealing, burglary, and being an accessory after the fact. They wanted her badly.

How did a girl like Maxine become friends with such a criminal? If she helped them, then they would help her. After all, she'd helped to kill an unborn baby and attempted to murder her man's mistress. Maxine would still go to jail, but they would charge her with involuntary homicide and not first-degree murder, which meant she could get paroled sooner.

As the detectives were preparing to allow Scottie to speak to his girlfriend, they received a phone call from the hospital. More grim news. The family had taken Sandy off life support, and she'd passed away less than an hour earlier. Now it was a double homicide.

Scottie went into the room to speak to Maxine. The moment she saw him, she burst into more tears. She was hoping he could work his magic to get her out.

Scottie smiled her way. He took a seat across from her, and the first thing he said to her was, "Don't worry, baby. I'm gonna hire you the best defense lawyer that money can buy."

"Defense lawyer?" Maxine didn't want to defend anything. She just wanted to go home. She wanted out of this nightmare. She did nothing. She didn't attack Sandy.

"It's terrible, baby. You fucked up," he said.

Maxine felt like she had no more tears to cry, because she had been crying since the nightmare started, but her eyes continued to leak. Scottie looked at her with hopelessness. Until this point, she thought he could turn water into wine. She loved him, and she always believed in him. He was smarter than the common thug. He had ambition, and he had money. But tonight Maxine saw him as a mere man. Perhaps he wasn't grasping her situation.

She leaned in closer to him and whispered, "They want me to tell them about Layla."

Scottie's jaw tightened. "Not here, not now." He motioned his head up toward the camera.

She whispered to him, "I already know about the camera, Scottie. I'm no fool. But we should talk. I don't know when I'll see you again, and I need you to tell me what to do."

"What you mean? You already know what to do. I've schooled you on this numerous times. You get knocked, you don't snitch. Period!"

Baffled, Maxine stared blankly at Scottie. Yes, that's what he always said to his goons and street soldiers, but she was his girlfriend. She didn't sell drugs or know anything incriminating about his drug empire. So, was "Don't snitch" directed toward her? This was different. This was murder. Maxine felt that Scottie thought she had actually killed Sandy over him.

"This isn't my fault. It wasn't me, Scottie. And if I tell them who it was, then they will let me go, right?"

Maxine had always valued her boyfriend's opinion. He wouldn't leave her to rot in jail. He'd come immediately upon hearing the news, so it meant he cared about her well-being.

Smoothly, Scottie extended his arms across the table and placed both his hands on hers. He locked eyes with his beautiful, innocent, frightened girlfriend. He looked at her deadpan and squeezed her hand so tight, he almost cut off her blood circulation.

Maxine didn't know what was going on or what to expect. She squirmed but didn't yelp out.

Scottie leaned in closer to her and gave her a soft kiss on the lips. Eyes to eyes, and inches from her face, he repeated, "Baby girl, we don't snitch—ever! You ride this out, and I promise you'll be home with me sooner than you think. You're innocent, I know it. Anyone can see that. Trust the system. I got you. Maybe we can get you off with a technicality on their end. Cops always fuck shit up."

The detectives were watching and hearing everything that was said. They allowed it to continue uninterrupted, thinking they could use it to their advantage, though it wasn't much.

Scottie ended his discussion with Maxine, kissed her lips again, and stepped out of the interrogation room. He put on a show, hoping that Maxine could hear him speaking about her rights. He screamed out, "Yo, why is my girl still here? Y'all know she ain't do nothing! She ain't got nothing to say to y'all."

The detectives cursed back, and he cursed back. They threatened him with arrest, but Scottie seemed unfazed by the threat. But he wasn't a stupid man. He would not be arrested too. He eventually left.

Maxine was disturbed by the visit and the commotion with Scottie and the cops.

Moments later, one of the detectives entered the room and took a seat before her. "Are you ready to talk now?"

Maxine believed in Scott, knowing he would do everything in his power to get her free. "No."

She finally invoked her right to have an attorney by her side, just as Scottie had always drilled his crew to do when arrested.

The detective huffed with frustration. She had been brainwashed by love and stupidity. "You're making a terrible mistake," he said. "We heard the conversation. He doesn't love you. He doesn't care about you at all."

She refused to listen. He knew nothing about her and Scottie's love.

Before departing, the detective turned with an afterthought for Maxine. "We had cops sitting on the location where your precious BMW was parked. You know before he came to visit you, he went to move that car? Then two hours later, he comes here. And that's a man who puts his woman first? It's your life, not ours."

It was all designed to provoke some rage out of Maxine, but she continued to sit there looking pitiful.

"You're too smart to be this dumb. And a man like him—he's probably fucking your best friend, Layla. The one he's making you protect."

Maxine shook her head vigorously, denying that either of them would ever hurt her in such a way. Maxine now didn't believe a word they had said to her about helping her get off. She didn't trust the police. She shut up and did as Scottie told her. Scottie had a lot of money, and he would pay for the best counsel. There was no way she could be convicted of a murder she didn't commit, right?

2014

The moment Meyer stepped foot in Delaware, he despised the place, finding it desolate and boring. He wanted to blow it all up. He lit a cigarette and took a needed drag, feeling despondent about the position Scott put them in. It felt like their father was punishing them.

"What Pop sees in this place, I don't know," Meyer said to Bugsy.

"He sees opportunity—money to be made," Bugsy replied.

Meyer chuckled.

"You find it funny?"

"He treats us like fuckin' puppets, Bugsy. We had our own thing happenin' in New York, and now he wants us to become New Jack City in fuckin' Delaware. Look at this place. What the fuck! I'm ready to shoot somebody just to have some fun," Meyer said loudly.

"You never have been a patient little brother—always the sound of thunder but never the lightning, not knowing when and how to strike."

"Spare me your fuckin' parables, Bugsy. And just because you were born ten minutes before me don't make you older."

Bugsy shook his head at his little brother. "You're an idiot."

"I'm an idiot? You wearin' a fuckin' nine-thousand-dollar suit in this hot-ass weather—what, look the part, be the part. Yeah, ayyite, you wannabe Frank Lucas muthafucka!"

Meyer took a few more drags from his cigarette and flicked it away. He then said, "What is there to do for fun around here anyway?"

"We need to start taking care of business," Bugsy mentioned.

"What? We just got into town. Fuck that! Pops sent us down here, but I ain't rushin' to do shit! Nigga, what I *do* need right now is a twenty sack and some fuckin' pussy. I had the sweetest piece of pussy in New York, and Pops gonna drag me away from it to this lame-lookin' fuckin' place."

The brothers stood next to Meyer's black Escalade in front of Ray's Market on North King Street in downtown Wilmington. The ninety-thousand-dollar truck was showroom-shiny on 26-inch chrome rims and fully loaded. They watched the activity around them. As late afternoon transitioned into early evening, the working crowd headed home, and the streets thickened with some traffic. Nothing like New York, though.

The brothers watched the fiends move about with the working crowd and civilians. They were like roaches in the kitchen, moving about freely even with the lights on.

"First thing we do is get with Lucky and talk to her," Bugsy suggested.

"Yeah, let's find her so I can personally thank her for the move down here. You know she gonna think she the boss of us, right? 'Cuz she mentioned this place to Pop and 'cuz she been down here with Whistler."

"She does her thing, and we do ours," Bugsy replied.

"And Pops calls *us* spoiled." Meyer chuckled. "Daddy's little girl, right?"

Bugsy didn't respond.

"Nigga, you ain't hungry?"

Bugsy shook his head. He was ready to leave. He had business on his mind and wanted to get their operation started in town.

"Well, I'm starving, nigga. I'm 'bout to get me some chicken. And don't ask me for any, nigga," Meyer said, approaching the chicken spot next door to Ray's Market.

"Don't take forever."

"Fuck me, nigga! Yes! Just like that! Oooh! Like that!"

On all fours, Lucky hollered in pleasure as Whistler slammed his erection into her pussy. He clutched her hips and opened her up with roughness and lubrication as he squeezed her cheeks and danced inside of her.

Lucky clutched the bed sheets and bit down on her bottom lip, loving every minute of it. She couldn't get enough of Whistler.

"You gonna make me fuckin' come!" Lucky announced.

She loved the way Whistler gripped the back of her neck as he worked her. Her body was ready to shake with an orgasm. She could feel the rush. His pinches on her nipples fanned the flames.

Lucky groaned and moaned. Doggy-style was one of her favorite positions.

She could feel every inch of him digging into her. "Fuck me, nigga! Ooooh shit! That dick gonna make me fuckin' come!" Just as she was about to explode and cream all over Whistler's erection, his cell phone rang and vibrated against the table.

Whistler slowed his thrust inside of her.

She barked, "Nigga, don't stop! Keep fuckin' me."

He let the call go to voice mail.

As they were about to get their rhythm going again, Lucky's phone rang. She became even more incensed. She wanted to finish.

Whistler stopped grinding inside of her, pulled out, and went to answer her phone, his dick swinging. Lucky was against it, but he felt it might be important. "Who this?"

"Nigga, this is Meyer, that's who. We on our way to y'all right now."

"Okay," Whistler replied.

Whistler didn't look too worried. He turned to Lucky and said, "Your brothers are on their way here."

"Shit!" Lucky removed herself from the bed. "They definitely got perfect timing—I was about to fuckin' come." Lucky scrambled to get dressed as she griped about the bedroom interruption. But she had to keep her affair with Whistler a secret. Her brothers would tell their father if they found out.

Whistler collected his things. He coolly got dressed and departed Lucky's room.

An hour later, Meyer, Bugsy, Lucky, Whistler, Luna, and several other goons held court in a room at the DoubleTree hotel on the outskirts of town. On one double bed was an assortment of weapons, from handguns to assault rifles and machine guns. Cigarette smoke filled the room.

Lucky sat at the edge of the second double bed, smoking a Newport. Whistler stood by the window, and the brothers were seated at the table.

"We already met with the detective and arranged something with him," Lucky said.

"Like what?" Meyer asked.

"A compromise," Lucky said.

"So you got things started without us. You the boss, huh?" Meyer said.

"We supposed to wait on you, Meyer? I don't even know why Pop sent y'all down here; we don't need any help with this."

Meyer laughed. "Obviously, he feels y'all do. And if you would have just kept your damn mouth shut and been content with business in New York, then we wouldn't be in this forsaken city."

"You got something to say to me, Meyer?" Lucky stood up from the bed and readied herself for a confrontation with her brother. "You never know when to shut the fuck up!"

Meyer lifted himself from his seat too, glaring at his little sister. "*You* make me shut the fuck up, little sis!"

"Enough!" Whistler stepped between the siblings, showing his authority. "Both of y'all, sit down and shut up."

Meyer and Lucky did what they were told, knowing not to go against their father's second-in-command.

"We're down here for a reason, and that reason is for expansion, nothing else. Now Scott sent you two boys down here for a reason, not to fight with your sister. We are an organization—a fuckin' dynasty—not some ordinary street gang ready to have a civil war."

Meyer frowned, not wanting to hear a speech from Whistler.

"Your father knows a good opportunity when he sees one. You think he would send his kids down here to set up shop if this wasn't profitable? He and Lucky see something in this city."

"So, what next then?" Meyer asked.

"I want you and your brother to sweat this fiend named Marty. Lucky will describe him to you. We subtly put the squeeze on DMC, hit them where it hurts, and they don't see us coming. We made an agreement with Detective Jones—no unnecessary violence or bloodshed in the area."

Meyer said, "What you mean, Whistler? We ain't gonna kill these muthafuckas? So they just gonna hand everything over to us on a silver platter? If it's gonna be that easy, why bring the muscle and the guns?"

Whistler stared at Meyer. The young boy was always mouthy and problematic. Locking eyes with Meyer, he said, "Before I was interrupted, and I'm saying this to everyone—our attack on DMC can't be loud and messy. We can't bring any negative attention to our organization. A small city like this . . . too many homicides will create public outcry, and the press will be all over it. Too many bodies will attract the feds, and that will be bad for business."

"So what do you want us to do then?" Luna didn't understand it. Murder and bloodshed were his forte. Why have him in Delaware if couldn't kill people?

Whistler had a solution. "We make the bodies disappear, or we move them to a different area. Anyhow, it's our arrangement with the detective, and it's a smart play."

Meyer shook his head from side to side. "That's a lot of work, Whistler. I mean, we gotta kill a nigga and move the body to appease some small-town cop? I mean, since when do we listen to fuckin' cops? C'mon, are they workin' for us, or are we workin' for them?"

"Meyer, just chill," Bugsy said.

"I mean, I had a good thing going on in New York until this bullshit."

"And if you want to continue that good thing in New York, youngblood, then I advise you do what your father and I tell you to do. Or, son or not, you'll be out in the cold," Whistler said.

"So we patsies now, huh? Last time I checked, I was a lieutenant in my father's organization," Meyer said.

"*Your father's* organization, youngblood—remember that," Whistler replied. "Meyer, you keep making this an issue, and soon you will become an issue."

Whistler had a look in his eyes that said Meyer was pushing his buttons and testing his patience. Son or no son of Scott, Whistler had no time to deal with his absurdity. His hard look toward the young prince was enough to intimidate Meyer into silence.

Whistler gave out commands to each man in the room, while Lucky played the background. It was Whistler's show. He had the experience and intelligence to know how to activate a hostile takeover and obliterate another drug crew from their territory.

Meyer and Bugsy were in charge of surveillance on the opposing crew. They would connect with their inside snitch, Marty, and work on gathering as much information possible to make their move covert. Luna was their muscle and clean-up man for the bodies that would fall once they moved into the territory and set up stash houses.

Lucky and Whistler would deal with Detective Jones and the political end of things.

Everything was set. They were ready to flood the streets of Wilmington with their superior heroin, cocaine, and meth. It was time to implement the hostile takeover before the DMC saw it coming. By the time they figured it out, it would be too late. Deuce and his crew didn't stand a chance.

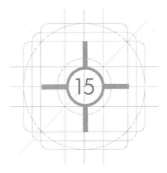

ayla lounged on the balcony of her lovely Florida home. The sun shined brightly down on her tanned body, creating a glistening effect on her light brown skin. She had a strong margarita nearby, and a burning blunt of potent Kush made her day even brighter. She took a few sips from her drink then took a few pulls of Kush as she relaxed. The house was quiet. Bonnie and Clyde were away doing their own thing, and Gotti was playing video games as usual.

Layla had fallen in love with the Sunshine State. The weather was fantastic, the ocean was picturesque, and the real estate was breathtaking. There was money in Florida. They called it the retirement state for a reason. Layla had plans to build something there. Something legitimate and large. The private complex she was building for her family was only the beginning. Real estate was gold, and she was ready to dig.

She took another puff and closed her eyes. The sun's heat beamed down on her. She lounged back on the convertible chaise and exhaled. Going from Brooklyn to Florida took a lot of hard work, climbing, sex, deceit, and death, but she did it. She felt she was that rose growing out of concrete. She was smirking down at those who'd doubted her—middle finger up at her enemies, and they could kiss her black ass. They hated on Layla in Brooklyn. Many felt that her position with Scott was unjust—that Maxine had gotten a raw deal, and Layla was to blame. But she was feared too, so not many people challenged her.

Layla had recently sent the fifteen thousand dollars for Maxine's benefit. It was the least she could do for a friend, though she hardly thought about Maxine until the inmate contacted or wrote her. It was a case of out of sight, out of mind. Layla had things to do, money to make, and her fabulous life to live.

She heard the weed-whacker start up below her. Fabian was performing his daily duties. He had been her gardener for several months. Having Fabian around was a quick distraction. He was a good worker, dedicated to his job, and, most of all, he was eye-candy.

Layla took a few sips of her margarita, lifted her body from the chaise, and walked toward the railing of her balcony. She gazed below and watched Fabian tend to her sprawling green lawn. He ran a successful landscaping company with over a dozen workers. Tall and broad, he had rock-hard arms and a mane of dreads that almost made him look animalistic. Her eyes were fixed on the beads of sweat on his shimmering dark skin as he worked on her lawn.

She breathed out with unrest, thinking about the things he could do to her and what she could do to him. She pictured him and his long dreads buried between her open legs, tasting her every nook and cranny like ice cream on a hot day. She wondered how it would feel to have him inside of her, his large hands cupping her ass and his mouth latched onto her nipples.

But there was no way she would ever act on the temptation. Scott would have him killed and then dismembered, with no hesitation. He had done it before. Scott had a very dangerous "jealous bone" with what was his, from his wife to his family.

⚬⚬⚬

Layla remembered Antonio from Crown Heights, Brooklyn. He was a tall, smooth, handsome, dark-skinned hustler with a thing for her. She was with Scott at the time, and they were the "it couple" in Brooklyn. Antonio was a dealer on the come-up, not afraid to fight for his respect and his business. Antonio went after what he wanted, including Layla. He didn't fear Scott. Though Scott was her man, Layla was fond of Antonio. He said all the right things, and there was something so attractive about him.

Layla just wanted to enjoy his company. She didn't expect things to go so far with him. She was playing with fire, enjoying the attention from both men, and she didn't expect to get burned so severely.

After months of sexual tension between her and Antonio, she finally gave in and gave him some pussy. The sex with Antonio was better than she expected it to be. It damn near blew her mind. Just like that, she was fucking two rivals.

Two months passed before Scott found out. A little birdie told him. He confronted Layla and beat her severely. Then he took her to a secret location where he had Antonio tied to a chair, butt naked and bleeding.

Scott made Layla watch as he viciously tortured Antonio. He and his goons did every horrific thing imaginable to him, including mutilate his genitals. Then they dismembered him.

"Look at him!" Scott instructed her.

Layla was in tears, afraid for her own life.

"This is what happens when you cross me. You're my woman, and don't you ever forget that!"

That incident became forever etched in her memory. Scott was crazy and dangerous. It was her one and only warning.

But Scott was a hypocrite. He was a womanizer, but he wanted Layla to behave herself. She gave him six kids, and he gave her the lifestyle of the rich and fabulous. She couldn't complain, although it was a troubled relationship.

Scott was over a thousand miles away in New York, and Layla suspected his infidelity. There were rumors about other women having children by him, but she had no proof. Scott had enough money and power to cover anything up. He was a handsome and powerful man, and so many ladies wanted him. There were a few he wanted back. Though Layla was his wife, sometimes, she felt like the mistress.

Fabian smelled the weed, looked up, and caught Layla getting lit. He smiled, wanting to partake in the illegal recreation, but she was the boss.

"Is it hot enough for you today?" she asked him.

"It is."

She smiled. "You want some of this bomb-ass Kush?" They stared at each other again; she could see him contemplating her offer.

"I'll pass, Mrs. West. I need to get these hedges trimmed," he said.

"Your loss."

Fabian went back to tending the bushes, and Layla pivoted and walked into the bedroom. The day was growing late, and she had some business to take care of.

Layla stepped out of her Florida home looking fabulous in an ivory lace mini-dress and raffia-detailed heels. With the top down on her Jaguar XK, she soared out of the driveway and headed toward the construction site. She was upset with the unexpected lack of progress in her development project.

Once again, she met with the site manager, Ron. There was an issue with the inspection, and she was becoming dismayed at the spiraling costs. She thought she had everything under control before construction. She had meticulously gone through the right channels, spoken to the right people, funded the right amounts, and paid off what needed to be paid. Scott wasn't around, so she had to put her boots on the ground and make moves. Now she was facing bureaucratic obstructions.

Layla climbed back into her Jaguar and headed to the city. She had a bone to pick with her property development consultant, Braxton Gambaro. He had twenty years in the business and was patient enough to explain the business to her. With a high cost. She was new at developing, but she had the money to buy up city blocks.

Layla parked in the garage under the twenty-two-story glass high-rise in the city. Gambaro was on the fifteenth floor. His office was professionally decorated with pieces of artwork from different countries—African masks, wooden sculptures, and vases. The dark furnishing blended in with the unusual patterns of décor to create a cohesive, unique atmosphere.

Layla took a seat in the leather armchair opposite Braxton's executive desk and high-back leather chair, while he talked on the phone. A balding white man of average height with piercing blue eyes, he was sharply dressed, articulate, and smart, and he had an infectious smile. Not to mention, an eye for business and real estate.

Braxton curtailed his phone conversation and smiled at Layla. "It's good to see you again, Mrs. West."

"Let's cut the formalities, Braxton, okay?" Layla replied sharply. "I just came from the construction site, and suddenly my site manager is telling me about a mountain of problems. What's going on? You're supposed to help me avoid these problems. I just wanna build something for my family down here and not go broke doing it."

"Cost overruns are the nature of the business, Layla. We talked about this," he replied.

"You keep telling me this, but I'm no fool, Braxton. I may be black and from Brooklyn, but I know what's goin' on here—Y'all wanna put the squeeze on me. How much?"

"Excuse me?" Braxton uttered, somewhat taken aback by her question.

"Braxton, you and I both now how things work—It takes a little extra somethin' to get somethin' done and done on time, right?"

"Mrs. West, are you implying that I bribe someone?"

"Look, I'm putting millions of dollars into this project for my family. Everybody always got their hand out lookin' for something, so let me just cut through the red tape and make it easier." Layla reached into her purse and removed a stack of hundred-dollar bills. She placed it on the center of Braxton's desk. "That's twenty-five thousand dollars. I don't want any issues, Braxton. No problems with the building inspectors, no issues with getting permits, and no problems with any unions. Do you feel me?"

Braxton stared at the cash on his desk. He took a deep breath, leaned forward in his chair, and picked up the money. Braxton Gambaro was a property developer at least marginally corrupt. Layla knew to come to him with her project because of his political influence in Florida and alleged ties to the mob.

"I feel you," Braxton said.

"Good." Layla stood up from her seat. "It's better to deal wit' me than to deal wit' my husband. He's a very dangerous man, an' he isn't as patient as I am."

She marched out of the man's office feeling confident there would be no more issues with her project.

Layla climbed into her Jaguar and sped out the parking garage. She needed to keep herself busy and focused, mainly because she was a horny bitch with no dick in her life. She was trying to live the fabulous life to the fullest, but her sex life was in shambles while Scott was away doing God-knows-what.

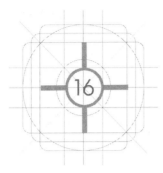

Meyer and Bugsy stared stone-faced at Marty and listened to him talk about Deuce and DMC. He was telling them everything he knew about the organization, including the locations of a few stash houses, the muscle they had protecting it, and how DMC did business.

Marty chain-smoked, feeling uneasy in their presence. Meyer was especially unnerving with his impatience with Marty, no matter how helpful he tried to be.

"Talk, nigga!" Meyer shouted. "You fuckin' dumb fiend! We look like we got all day for you to tell us something?"

"I'm-I'm sorry," Marty stammered.

"Muthafucka, don't be sorry. Open your fuckin' druggie-ass mouth and do your job, nigga!"

Marty fretfully took a drag from his cigarette and glanced at Bugsy and Luna. They were quiet, allowing Meyer to humiliate him. These dudes looked like they could tear him apart if something went wrong or if they didn't believe him.

Meyer frowned. He wanted to put out his Newport in Marty's eye. He didn't care about anyone's feelings. He continued his taunt. "Nigga, we still waitin' to hear something from you. Do I gotta slap you? Huh?"

Marty said, "Their main dude is Rock; he's the town drug dealer that cops from DMC."

"What's he moving?" Bugsy asked. "And how many kilos?"

"He's 'bout that powder, both brown an' white. Don't know the exact amount of ki's he's moving," Marty said.

"We need to get at that nigga and fuck his world up," Meyer said.

"Remember Whistler's instruction—No unnecessary violence. We do things chill and discreet," Bugsy reminded Meyer.

"So we just sit back and play like the police? Do surveillance on these muthafuckas and take notes, huh? What? We gonna fuckin' indict them on charges? We came down here to make moves, not sit on our asses and play scared!"

"When we move, we gonna move correctly, Meyer. There's still a lot to learn about this group," Bugsy said.

"What the fuck more is there to learn, Bugsy? It's been a fuckin' week now, and we just lounging around lookin' fuckin' crazy. I'm about to lose my fuckin' mind," Meyer griped.

"We continue to watch them and learn more about them," Bugsy said.

"And who made you the fuckin' boss over me, huh?" Meyer stepped closer to his brother with a dark frown.

"Fall back, Meyer," Bugsy warned.

"Or what, bro? Huh? You gonna run and tell Pop? That's what you gonna do? You his little bitch, or better yet, you Whistler's bitch, right? When we ain't around, you get on your knees and suck his dick, right? Play nice with him and shit? Tickle his balls to give him some encouragement?"

Bugsy scowled and clenched his fists. He didn't avert his look from Meyer. He was intimidating, but Bugsy had the same fierce pedigree. The disrespect was uncalled for. Bugsy did his best to keep his composure, but Meyer knew how to push his buttons.

"You finished with your little tantrum, *little brother*?" Bugsy replied.

"I'm fuckin' tired of this shit." Meyer sucked his teeth. "This sneakin' around, watchin' shit, and takin' fuckin' pictures—we lookin' like roaches in the fuckin' dark."

"We do this right, or we don't do it at all," Bugsy said.

Meyer sighed heavily. "Y'all got a nigga fuckin' stressed out. Yo, I'm fuckin' some bitch tonight. I don't give a fuck."

"Continue, Marty," Bugsy said. "And sorry for the interruption."

Meyer blew out his mouth. "Yo, what the fuck you apologizing to this fuckin' fiend for? Huh? Who the fuck is this nigga for you to be apologizin' to? He a bum nigga!"

"I'm just tryin' to work wit' ya," Marty said.

"Yo, shut the fuck up!" Meyer screamed. "In fact, get the fuck out my face, nigga!" He rushed over and pushed Marty violently to the ground.

Marty landed roughly on his side and scraped his elbow from the fall.

Meyer stood over him and spat on him. "You get up when I say you can get up!"

Bugsy asked, "Is all that called for?"

"We ain't being violent out there. Shit, my aggression gotta go somewhere."

"You're an idiot," Bugsy said.

"Fuck you, nigga!"

Luna stood to the side smoking a cigarette and looking demonic. He didn't interfere with family arguments.

Just as things were getting out of hand, Bugsy's cell phone rang.

"I need to take this, little brother. It's Whistler," Bugsy said almost mockingly, stepping away from Meyer.

Marty remained on the floor, not wanting to anger Meyer.

They'd been in Delaware for a week, and they'd not yet seen any action. Whistler's instruction was to observe then report and plan. Keep things quiet and subtle. He was in New York with their father dealing with other business, while the lieutenants were doing the tedious job of surveillance and learning the way things worked with the rival crew.

The brothers moved around town in an unassuming dark blue Ford Bronco with Marty as their guide. They were observing how members of DMC moved. They took down the dates and times of particular activities and watched drug dealers and other members operate from afar. Bugsy even snapped pictures of some of the activity and the cars they drove.

DMC's setup was smart. They rarely talked on the phones, and when they did, everything was said in code. Most meetings were face to face, and they frequently changed up, moving the locations of certain stash houses to confuse law enforcement and stickup crews. Their security was tight and their dealings nomadic, so it was hard for anyone to get the drop on them.

The stash house on Pine Street was one of their busiest. The location on N. Jefferson Street was saturated with townhouses and working people. The house on N. Jefferson Street seemed the easiest to go after. There wasn't much traffic around, and it was near the I-95 expressway.

It was late evening and hot. Bugsy sat behind the wheel of the Bronco, Meyer sat shotgun, and Luna was in the back seat. They'd been watching the place for three days. Rock ran both stash houses, so he was their primary focus.

A black Lexus came to a stop in front of the townhouse, and Rock stepped out dripping in jewelry and wearing nice clothing, looking the part of a high-end drug dealer. Rock was a young, portly African American with starting dreads. He was on his cell phone, speaking in code, unaware he was being watched.

They observed Rock go into the townhouse. He stayed inside for several minutes before coming back out, jumping into his Lexus, and driving off.

Bugsy followed him closely but subtly for several miles. He eventually ended up at Canby Park off Maryland Avenue.

Rock was to meet up with two Maryland hustlers named Black Sean and Rasun. He had been their supplier for little over a year, and his operation with them was simple. To ensure he never got caught with a large quantity of narcotics, he would meet with his clients and give them an address face to face. It was a different address twice a month. Black Sean and Rasun would drive to the location and retrieve several kilos for street distribution. Everything was built on trust with them.

Rock pulled into the parking lot of the park and waited.

Luna and the brothers were close by, watching his every movement. Five minutes passed, and they soon noticed a Tahoe drive into the park and park near Rock.

"Bingo!" Meyer was excited to see some activity happening.

Black Sean climbed out of the SUV and climbed in Rock's Lexus.

A few moments passed, and Black Sean exited the Lexus and jumped back into the Tahoe. Black Sean had the location to pick up five kilos of heroin that he'd already paid for. The meeting with Rock was prompt and straightforward.

Bugsy followed the Tahoe with the two men, since they already knew Rock's movements and locations. They drove for miles before they arrived at the Colony North Apartments.

In the parking lot, Rasun exited the Tahoe with his gun concealed in his waistband and went into the building to pick up the product. It was being maintained by one of Rock's trusted crew members.

Black Sean remained seated in the Tahoe. He was armed, but he was relaxed, having done the routine so many times without incident. He smoked a cigarette and waited for his partner in crime to step out the building with the ki's.

For the brothers, it was now or never. They were in the same parking lot ready to strike. Meyer and Luna cocked back their weapons and exited the Bronco. Meyer was itching to take care of business, but Whistler had warned them to keep things on the sly without any unnecessary violence.

While Black Sean smoked his Newport in the driver's seat, Meyer and Luna emerged at him with swiftness.

Meyer thrust the barrel of his 9mm into the man's face, stunning him. "You move, nigga, and I'll blow your fuckin' head off right now," Meyer exclaimed.

Black Sean scowled. "I'm cool."

They disarmed him and joined him inside the Tahoe, holding him at gunpoint. They laid low in the back seat of the SUV, ready for Rasun to come out the building with the kilos.

"Stay cool, nigga, and you get to see tomorrow," Meyer said.

Black Sean remained still and upset. He had been caught slipping. Meyer had the gun to the back of his neck, his finger on the trigger, as they waited for his partner to come out the building.

Bugsy sat in the Ford watching it all go down. In case things didn't go as expected, he was ready to let loose the cannon he had in his hand—a .50-cal. The gun could bring a charging elephant down.

"How long this nigga gonna be?" Meyer asked.

"He'll be out soon. Just chill," Black Sean replied.

"Nigga, don't fuckin' tell me to chill!" Meyer growled, pushing the gun against the back of Black Sean's skull.

Black Sean sat still and uneasy. There was no way he could get the drop on Meyer and Luna. And how could he warn Rasun without getting his head blown off? He knew the two stickup men were dangerous. He'd been in the game long enough to recognize a viable threat.

The look in Meyer's eyes was almost satanic. His eyes were bloodthirsty, and his movements were certifiable. Black Sean just stared straight ahead, not knowing if he would live or die. They didn't wear masks, which made the situation a lot scarier for him. Usually when men didn't wear masks, they didn't plan on leaving behind any witnesses. When he saw Rasun exiting the building, he felt things were about to get a lot more serious.

Rasun walked toward the truck carrying a black book bag large enough for the five kilos.

Black Sean heard the clicking to the pistol, indicating a bullet could soon be cut loose into his flesh. He took a nervous deep breath, feeling defenseless and defeated.

Meyer and Luna were ready for his partner. The passenger door opened, and Rasun climbed into the seat unaware of the danger.

The moment Rasun was inside the truck, Luna pounced on him, pistol-whipping him severely. "Ask me if it's loaded, bitch!" He shoved the gun into Rasun's face while violently restraining him.

Black Sean scowled and gritted his teeth, wanting to help Rasun, but there wasn't anything he could do about it. He angrily uttered, "Y'all know who you stealin' from?"

"We know, muthafucka!" Meyer retorted and then bashed the pistol against his head, spewing blood. "Drive, nigga—nice and slow. We goin' for a nice ride."

Black Sean reluctantly started the SUV and put it into reverse. He slowly backed out of the parking spot and drove away coolly.

Meyer instructed Black Sean, "Drive toward the freeway."

It was daybreak, with the sun freshly rising in the sky. It was gradually becoming the start of a new day in the DMV area (DC, Maryland, and Virginia). It would be another scorching day, with the weatherman predicting temperatures soaring to 99 degrees with oppressive humidity. Rush-hour traffic was piling up on the highways, especially I-95 going south into DC.

Two miles from the highway, on an isolated road in Maryland, a state trooper pulled behind what appeared to be abandoned vehicle on the shoulder of the road. The truck had Maryland plates, dark tints, and chrome rims. The trooper saw no activity inside the Tahoe. He quickly ran the plates, and they came back clean. He climbed out of his car and cautiously approached the truck with his hand near his holstered gun. He took a peek into the front seat but saw no one or anything unusual. He continued to look into the truck, making his way toward the rear, and what he saw shocked him. Stuffed in the back of the truck were two bodies contorted against each other. The stunned trooper quickly called it in.

A half-hour later, homicide detectives opened the rear door to the Tahoe, and there were Black Sean and Rasun. Dead. Both men had been shot in the head execution-style. The cops found no drugs. The killers wanted DMC to think that the two men were ambushed in their own town and never made it to Delaware.

1995

Maxine fidgeted in her chair next to Fred Chesney, one of the best criminal attorneys in the city. She was quiet and nervous, dressed in a white top under a gray blazer and matching knee-length skirt. She looked sophisticated and innocent, playing the role of an intelligent young girl who didn't get into trouble.

This was the big day. A jury of her peers had finally reached a verdict, and in a moment, her fate would be revealed. Her trial had lasted a grueling two weeks, and the courtroom was semi crowded. The prosecutor, Natalie Knight, was an adept lawyer with a ninety percent conviction rate. She was a savage pit bull in the courtroom, calling Maxine everything from a baby killer to a common criminal, to which her defense attorney strongly objected.

Fred and Natalie went back and forth in the courtroom with heated arguments. It was like *Matlock*. Fred presented Maxine to the jury as an educated, decent, and innocent college girl from a good Christian family who attended church regularly. He wanted the jury to know that she had no criminal record and had never been arrested. She had a bright future ahead of her; she was a law student herself, so why would she murder Sandy? Fred Chesney painted the perfect picture of his client to the jury. Almost made it look like she was Mother Teresa herself.

But the prosecution had a motive for the attack and murder. Natalie Knight painted Maxine as a jealous bitch in love with a thug named Scottie, who would do anything and everything to keep her man. The prosecutor stated to the jury that Sandy's pregnancy with Scottie sent the defendant over the edge, and she snapped. Sandy was a threat to Maxine's relationship. Witnesses testified against Maxine and brought up the previous run-in between Sandy and Maxine at the bodega.

Fred refuted the witnesses' statements, saying Sandy was the aggressor that day, not Maxine. He said it was self-defense and that Sandy was a bully, even when she was pregnant. Maxine had the right to defend herself.

It was a war, and Maxine's freedom was on the line.

Maxine took the stand in her defense. It was a risky move, but Maxine felt confident that she could persuade the jury and everyone else about that day. She wanted to tell them from her own mouth she was innocent. Her lawyer felt she would be okay on the stand since she was educated and smart. He questioned her, and she was coherent. No street slang came from her mouth, and she held eye contact.

The prosecutor was hungry to sink her teeth into her. Natalie didn't play nice. Everything about Maxine came into play, from her relationship with Scottie the drug dealer to her friendship with Layla. Natalie Knight explained to the jury that there was more to Maxine than met the eye. She grilled Maxine about the night of the murder. Why was she there? She opposed the self-defense theory, proclaiming that Maxine had been stalking Sandy.

Her defense attorney immediately shouted out, "Objection," and stated his cause.

"Sustained," the judge announced.

The cross-examination from the prosecutor went on tirelessly, as Natalie tried to break down the defendant's character. Time after time, Maxine's lawyer would call out, "Objection!"

Maxine testifying on the stand could have been a hit or miss to the jury, who sat there listening intently to everything being said. She wondered what they thought about her. Did she do a good job defending herself from the she-wolf that repeatedly attacked her character and was calling her a cold-blooded murderer?

Now the trial was coming to an end, and Maxine wanted to jump through a window and fly away. She wanted to see daylight again. She had been locked down for several months. At her arraignment, the judge had denied her bail, and she had been remanded. It was a double homicide—a pregnant woman had been attacked and killed, along with the baby.

Maxine glanced behind her and saw her parents in attendance. Seeing them always there brought a slight smile to her face. They'd been supportive of her since day one. They spoke out about her being innocent. They prayed every day and defended Maxine's character being attacked.

Also seated in the courtroom on the day of her verdict was Scottie. He looked handsome and confident that she would beat the charge and would be acquitted of murder. He'd hired the best lawyer for Maxine with his drug money. He wanted to show her he had her back fully. When the two locked eyes, he winked at her and smiled.

The verdict came in after several hours of deliberation. This was it. They had a unanimous decision. The tension inside the courtroom was thick. The jury was back in their assigned seats, and none of them looked Maxine's way.

The judge took over the courtroom with his gavel and authority. He gazed at the jury and asked, "Do you have a verdict?"

The foreman of the jury stood up. "We do, Your Honor."

The judge was the first to see the verdict. His expression remained stoic.

Maxine and her attorney were to stand as she was to be read her fate. The feeling of trepidation continued to balloon inside her. She gazed at the jurors, feeling her heart beat a million times per second. She felt it beat so loud that it almost drowned out what anyone else had to say. She said a quick prayer.

"The Superior Court of New York, Kings County, in the matter of the people of the state of New York vs. Maxine Henderson, case number BA097345, we the jury in the above of title action find the defendant, Maxine Henderson, guilty of first-degree murder," the foreman proclaimed.

Maxine shrieked once she heard the word *guilty*. She was in absolute shock and denial. Her knees weakened, and she was about to hyperventilate. No, this wasn't happening. How did they find her guilty of first-degree murder? She wasn't a killer.

Immediately, tears trickled from her eyes, and she looked to her attorney for an explanation. But he was equally shocked.

Her parents cried in the courtroom. Her mother thrust herself into her husband's arms and sobbed.

Scottie's heart dropped into his stomach when he heard the guilty verdict. If only the jurors knew Maxine like he knew her. But with a bloody gun on the scene, her fingerprints, motive, and the mystery woman that Maxine refused to give up, there was only so much a lawyer could do. He'd tried, and he failed.

The self-defense argument didn't ring true to the jury. Numerous people had testified there was another person at the scene, but Maxine swore it was only her. The jury saw her as a manipulative liar who went to seek revenge and ultimately she got what she wanted, which was to have the woman carrying her fiancé's baby dead.

Maxine was about to be taken away into state custody. Fred felt there was still a fight. He promised that they would immediately appeal the verdict to the local court of appeals. It wasn't over.

Maxine was a complete mess. Her tears came harder and faster, as her face flooded with anguish. She thought about suicide. There was no way in hell her life had been flushed down the toilet and she was about to serve time for a crime she didn't commit. She couldn't hug her parents or kiss Scottie goodbye. They placed her in handcuffs and shackles and escorted her into lockup.

After the trial, a few jurors were interviewed, and they all said the same thing. Maxine's fiancé Scottie sitting in the courtroom with his expensive jewels, diamond watches, and his urban gear screamed out drug dealer to them. He hurt Maxine's case. If she was engaged to the drug-dealing thug, then the picture the defense was trying to paint of her was marred.

At her sentencing, Maxine was told she would spend the next twenty-five years to life in prison. It was a compromised verdict. Because she had never been in trouble before and the crime was over her fiancé, some suggested that she wouldn't be a complete threat to society.

The judge felt she deserved a shot at rehabilitation; therefore, she didn't receive life without the possibility of parole.

Either way, Maxine felt her life was over. Twenty-five years was a long time. There was no more home, no more normal life for her. She was now an inmate—state property.

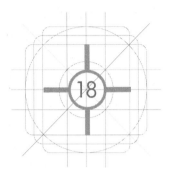

18

2014

Rock didn't know what happened to Black Sean and Rasun. He believed business went smoothly as usual. After the transaction, he celebrated with a few drinks at the strip club, made it rain on a few strippers, and later left with a voluptuous stripper named Candy for some extracurricular activities. In his personalized bedroom, they fucked passionately until they came and passed out, twisted together in exhaustion.

The next morning, Rock was awakened to the cold steel of a pistol against his forehead and several niggas standing in his bedroom.

He popped up wide-eyed. "What the fuck, yo! What y'all niggas want?" he hollered, panic in his voice.

"Chill, nigga," Meyer said.

Bugsy said, "We came to talk."

"Talk about what?"

"Tell the bitch to leave," Meyer said of the butt-naked Candy sleeping against him.

Rock quickly stirred her awake.

When she finally opened her eyes, she too was devastated to see the sudden threat surrounding them. "Ohmygod!"

Meyer yelled, "Bitch, get your shit and leave before you get murdered up in here!"

The look on Candy's face was one of candid fear. She leaped from the bed, hastily collected her things, and departed the bedroom faster than anyone could blink.

Bugsy tossed a few pictures onto the bed for Rock to see. A picture was worth a thousand words, and these images would start their conversation with Rock.

Rock was taken aback by the images of Black Sean and Rasun stuffed into the back of their Tahoe, both with large holes in their heads.

Bugsy said coolly, "I assume that we now have your complete attention."

"What is it that y'all want from me?"

"It's simple—your cooperation," Bugsy said.

"Y'all come into my bedroom uninvited and show me pictures of two of my regulars dead? What the fuck!"

Meyer took a seat at the foot of the bed, making himself comfortable.

Bugsy tossed an eight ball of their product toward Rock and said, "From now on, you cop from us."

"What?" Rock was baffled by their demand. "You know who I'm with?"

Meyer said, "DMC, right? Fuck them niggas!"

"Our product is far superior to DMC's shit," Bugsy said.

Rock examined the eight ball and shook his head. "They'll kill me."

"And who do you think we are? Some off-brand niggas that just came into town rolling the dice for fun? Nah, nigga. Check our fuckin' pedigree—You need to be more worried about us than them clown-ass niggas. We're official niggas rolling into your city, taking shit over. Put it like this—DMC is a mom-and-pop store, and we're fuckin' Wal-Mart, nigga, every fuckin' where. Ain't no stoppin' us," Meyer proclaimed.

"We already infiltrated the police. Detective Jones, that's Deuce's main guy on the force. Am I correct?" Bugsy said.

Rock slightly nodded.

"And there's Marty, the low nigga on the totem pole. There's Jimmy, Deuce's right-hand man, and then there is Jo-Jo and McCall, his top two enforcers. Deuce gets his supply from the Jamaicans in DC, and their product is low grade, and y'all have to cut it too many times to get a rise," Bugsy said. "Should I go on?"

"No," Rock muttered, shocked at what they knew.

Bugsy paused for a beat, allowing Rock to take it all in. "Listen, we're not here to kill you. We just want to talk business. Simple. Our offer will be a lot more generous than Deuce's. And you'll be compensated for your time and loss of men. But most important, you'll be part of a larger organization—one that comes with lawyers and political connections. Our organization takes pride in loyalty. We're subtle, but swift with violence when we need to be. And when you're with us, you're with us, and we're with you," Bugsy said, sounding like he was trying to sell him a new car.

Bugsy continued to sell a dream. "What you hold there will have your drug users swarming to get a taste."

Rock clutched the eight ball, looking at the heroin carefully. He knew there was no way out. Bugsy was giving him an offer he couldn't refuse.

Meyer said, "Deuce is on his way out, so now's the time to get on board. Like Beanie Sigel said, you either get down, or you lay down."

"My mamma ain't raise any fool," Rock said, "so I'll get down."

"See, I knew you were a smart man," Meyer said.

"One thing, though," Rock said.

"What the fuck you want, nigga?" Meyer asked, waving the gun at him.

"Chill, Meyer," Bugsy said. "Let him speak."

"Y'all gotta protect me from Deuce," Rock stated. "He's gonna come after me once he finds out about this, and he's nobody to fuck wit'. I'm telling you, Deuce and his goons—they're like nothing I ever seen before."

Meyer snarled. "Yo, y'all give this nigga too much fuckin' credit in this fuckin' town. If he was in New York, you know what that nigga would be? Dog food, nigga! He would be eaten alive by the real niggas in my town."

Bugsy said to Rock, "Let me reiterate to you, when you're with us, you're with us, and don't worry about Deuce. He's already being taken care of."

"It's gonna hit the fan nasty and hard. Deuce ain't gonna go down easily."

"Listen, you paranoid nigga, we done took down men much scarier and smarter than this Deuce muthafucka. I'm tired of hearing about this nigga like he some boogeyman that can't die. Nigga, everybody bleeds when they get shot in the fuckin' head!"

"Meyer, chill," Bugsy said.

Meyer was ready to hunt Deuce himself and kill him in a nasty way. It bothered him that the people in Delaware talked about him like he was a legend. He'd never heard the name in New York. As far as Meyer was concerned, Deuce was a weak nigga living on borrowed time. He was ready to become the star in town. He wanted muthafuckas to fear his name and status there like they did in NYC. Now he found his reason to be in Delaware. He was there not just for profit, but for recognition too. It was becoming an ego thing.

With their business completed, the men coolly exited the bedroom, leaving Rock behind with a lot to think about.

Immediately, Rock got up from his bed, locked his doors, and armed himself with several guns. He had just betrayed the devil he'd been dealing with. Deuce would find out everything somehow, and he would come for everyone, including him. Rock felt that the town would be turned into a war zone when these two clans inevitably clashed, and Wilmington would become a living hell for many people.

Rotting inside a female penitentiary for nearly twenty years gave Maxine a lot to think about. The reading of the guilty verdict replayed in her head over and over. That day defeated her both physically and mentally. She would never forget the look of heartbreak on her parents' faces when the guards dragged her back into jail. Her folks were crushed; they cried too. Scott quietly walked out of the courtroom. Max guessed he too was shocked by the verdict.

Maxine missed her parents so much. Early on in her sentence, they would come and visit her, but as the years went on, their visits dwindled. The farther south she was transferred, the more scarce the visitation had become. She had learned that her father had become ill. And she could do nothing for him.

To escape the pain, Maxine had to become Max, and she had to forget about her previous life. Her alter ego surfaced, and violence and drugs became a way to escape. She went from a good girl to a hardcore bitch. For twenty years, the rage inside her boiled until her blood turned into hot, molten lava.

While she remained caged, Layla started a family and became prosperous. Maxine always wanted that for herself. She wanted to give her parents grandchildren. She wanted the big, beautiful house with the white picket fence and green backyard, maybe with a pool and a few pets. She wanted a husband and a career. She wanted to live the American dream, but her conviction made sure it would never happen.

Max sat on her cot staring at a picture of Layla and Scott together. She felt played and humiliated by them both. She ripped the picture in half and crumpled it in her fist. Now was the time. No more feeling sorry for herself and taking her pain out on the other inmates.

With Shiniquia's help, she would have her justice. One by one, Layla and Scottie's kids would be knocked off, like their namesakes. First on her list was the youngest—nine-year-old Gotti. Max found it amusing and stupid that Layla would name all of her kids after legendary gangsters. How typical. *Gotti. What a joke!* Max figured since they wanted to name their children after gangsters, then they would die like gangsters.

She remembered when the real John Gotti's son, Frankie Gotti, was on his bicycle when he was accidentally mowed down and killed by a neighbor. This time, young Gotti's death would not be an accident.

Shiniquia joined Max in her jail cell. She took a seat next to her and slyly passed her a small stack of twenty-dollar bills. "All the payments are right on time from everyone."

"Cool." Max counted the cash, and it was over three hundred dollars. "I got Mark bringing in another batch next week—same style, same way."

"Can't wait. The girls are itching for another taste."

Mark was a dirty guard Max had under her thumb. For some extra cash on the side, he smuggled drugs into the prison for Max and Shiniquia to sell to the inmates. Mark also enjoyed the perks of being a male guard in a female prison.

On the side, Max was pimping a few girls to the male guards, including Mark. It was easy money, since several guards, the majority of whom were white, had a penchant for black girls. Max figured out a way to benefit from both the drugs and the girls. Many girls got high, so she would give them a discount on the drugs she sold if they agreed to have sex with the guard that desired them. For a taste of narcotics, the girls would link up with the guard that favored them, and they would quickly have oral sex or fuck in a separate room while there was a lookout. Both parties would get what they wanted. Max even supplied the condoms, which she had someone smuggle in for her. The last thing she needed was for one of the girls to get pregnant by a male guard. If that were to happen, it would spark an investigation and turn everything topsy-turvy. She couldn't afford any hiccups in her operation. She had worked hard to get where she was, and she had big plans.

"What about that other thing with your brother Wacka? Did the money come yet?"

"I haven't spoken to him yet, but it should be there," Shiniquia said.

"I need this to happen soon. And I want it to happen the way I described—by car—and make it ugly."

"Oh, wit' Wacka, it will be ugly. For what you got that bitch paying out, my brother don't got morals. He don't give a fuck if it's a kid or not, he gonna get the job done."

That was what Max wanted to hear. She needed a hardcore goon for what she had planned.

One by one, they would go, and Layla and Scott would soon know what it felt like to be helpless. There was no amount of money or power in the world to prevent their children's demise and, subsequently, theirs.

It was after midnight, and besides the TV playing, the remainder of the house was quiet. Wacka sat shirtless on the plush couch in the living room, his elbows pressed against his knees. He stared attentively at the large flat-screen mounted on the wall as he watched an episode of *Love and Hip Hop: Atlanta*. Wacka laughed at the fights and enjoyed the beautiful ladies on the screen. Their cattiness was amusing to him. They had a style and charisma about them that made him a fan of the show. Wacka would lick these bitches from head to toe and stick his tongue deep up the crack of their ass. Especially Karlie Redd, the black-haired beauty. Something about her made him go crazy.

"Yeah, I would definitely get that bitch pregnant," he said to no one.

He took a few sips of the cold beer in his hand, leaned back against the couch, and stretched his arms across the back. He was enjoying the neat, well-decorated house, which had all the latest amenities.

After the show was over, Wacka felt it was time to do what he came there to do. He'd spent too much time watching the TV show and fantasizing over Karlie Redd. But it wasn't like he was in any rush. Wacka was his own boss, and he did whatever the fuck he wanted to do.

He finished the beer and tossed it to the side. He stood up. At six two, his appearance was intimidating. He was dark-skinned and muscular with a shiny bald head and dark eyes. His upper torso was painted with tattoos—everything from gang-related to prison tats. Covering his back was a giant, highly detailed demonic skull covered in blood. His tattoos and his scars told his story—He was an absolute bad ass who gave no fuck about anyone or anything. Many thought he was a few cents short of a dollar.

Wacka picked up the large 8-inch bowie knife by his side and looked to his left. He scowled at two of his male captives gagged and hogtied on the floor.

He approached, and the two men squirmed and muttered something incoherent. It was their home and their goodies that Wacka had treated himself to. He raided their fridge, ate their food, and enjoyed their entertainment system for over an hour while the two men were tied up.

Wacka had broken into their home and held them at gunpoint. But these people weren't innocent civilians; they were known drug traffickers living the good life in DC. They too were dangerous men, and if the shoe were on the other foot, Wacka would have been a dead man in the blink of an eye. These people had ordered hits, destroyed lives, and were killers too. But Wacka had gotten the best of them. After stalking them for weeks, watching and learning everything about them, he made his move when they least expected it.

He crouched near Tommy, put the knife to his cheek, and said, "Y'all niggas comfortable?"

Tommy fidgeted in his restraints and muttered something incoherent again.

"What was that, nigga? Huh? Continue to make myself at home? I'm welcome here? Oh, your bitch is my bitch. That is so generous, Tommy. I appreciate the offer," Wacka said. "And you do have a gorgeous bitch."

Wacka didn't want to kill them yet. He was having some fun with them. He stood up and walked away.

Tommy and his brother watched him with fretful gazes. Their eyes followed him until he disappeared into the next room.

Wacka came back into the living room with Amber, Tommy's wife. She had duct-tape over her mouth, and she was trembling in Wacka's clutch.

"You know I'm very grateful that you would give me your wife. And they say you're a stingy and selfish bastard. I beg to differ," Wacka mocked.

Tommy and his brother squirmed against their stomachs, desperate to break free and help Amber.

Wacka placed the knife to Amber's throat. "Bitch, you gonna die slowly."

The blade nicked the side of her neck and drew some blood. For good measure, Wacka struck her with a violent blow.

Just then, his cell phone rang. He answered the call from Dagmar, one of his trusted cohorts.

"Wack," Dagmar called him for short, "that thing wit' your sister? It went through. The money came correct."

"That's what up. I need that. I guess we're taking a road trip south to Florida."

"Fo' sure, my nigga."

Wacka ended the call and went back to what he started before the interruption. With one quick motion, Wacka put the bowie knife to Amber's neck and cut her throat right there as she lay on her back in anguish. He watched as her blood pooled underneath her, crimson staining the wood flooring. Wacka could hear Tommy's gag-muffled screams of pain and agony as his wife's body lay lifeless nearby.

Tommy and his brother fidgeted harder, but to no avail. They weren't going anywhere while hogtied. They were at Wacka's mercy, though they believed there would be none tonight.

Wacka went to Tommy's brother first. He crouched near him and slowly placed the knife to his throat. The brother cringed, knowing his fate. His breathing was labored, and his movement strictly limited.

"It's been fun, but life goes on, right?" Wacka taunted him. With that, he sliced from left to right, opening the man's throat. Blood sprayed on the floor like a fountain, and the life drained from his eyes. He died soon after.

Tommy's eyes were watery. It wasn't supposed to end like this for him. He could shout no last words to Wacka—no threats or insults.

Wacka crouched over him in a threatening stance and placed the knife to his neck before repeating the slashing motion against Tommy's neck from left to right. Tommy choked on his own blood. It took a moment for him to finally die.

Wacka exhaled and admired his work. Three dead, now it was time to collect. He went into the kitchen and rinsed the blood from his black latex gloves. Then he went into the next room and placed two kilos of heroin into a bag. It was enough for him to eat off of. Maybe he'd wholesale it out of town or retail it on the street. Either way, it was a lot of money. Tommy and his brother were known around town as the moneymakers, the big shots, moving kilos like running water. Wacka gathered jewelry, cash, and a few guns after he secured the heroin. It was a good payday for him.

Wacka made sure not to leave any evidence behind—no DNA, no fingerprints. The gloves would stay on until he left the premises. The bodies would stay there and rot until they were found. He left the place feeling no remorse. It was what he did best—kill people and take their shit.

Wacka was ready for a road trip. It would be a good idea to get out of town for a while anyway. He knew the deaths of Tommy and his brother would stir up some chaos in DC, but he wasn't running scared. He had to do a job his sister had connected him with. He didn't care who it was. If the contractor was paying good money, he would go after the president of the United States.

20

Layla lay on her bed, sleeping in late that morning. It was another sunny, sizzling day in Florida, and she had a slight hangover. She had gone out clubbing the night before, gotten her drink on, and mingled with a few people. All she wanted to do was sleep all morning and perhaps all afternoon. She could afford to sleep all day. Her husband wasn't home, her kids entertained themselves, and her business was taken care of.

Gotti was a handsome young boy, athletic and the spitting image of his father. If he wasn't playing video games, then he'd be in the pool or messing around with his friends and their high-end toys and expensive bicycles. Gotti was a spoiled brat who got whatever he wanted and did whatever he wanted. His father was Scott West.

Gotti and his friends ran around the pool area playing tag and pushing each other into the pool. It was all for laughs. They kicked each other playfully and tossed around food in jest.

Gotti did a back flip off the deck and landed into the water, creating an impressive splash. He was a good swimmer. Layla had gotten him swimming lessons when he was four years old. Now nine, he was looking like Michael Phelps in the water. His friends tried to follow his lead, but they landed awkwardly in the pool. They weren't as good as Gotti. They played Marco Polo and tossed toys and other items into the pool just for fun. They didn't care who had to clean up behind them. They were boys being boys.

They soon became bored with the pool.

"Let's go ride our bikes," one of Gotti's friends suggested.

They were all with it.

Gotti had a new bicycle he wanted to show off to his buddies. A one of a kind. His father had paid three thousand dollars for it. He wanted to explore the neighborhood with his friends, so they could race their bikes and pop wheelies in the street. He quickly dried off and went inside the house to ask his mother if he could go.

Layla wanted complete silence while she lounged in her bedroom and slept. A sudden knocking on her door almost sent her into a heated rage.

"What?!" she screamed out.

"Mommy, can I go bike-riding with my friends around the neighborhood?" Gotti asked.

"What! Hell no. Go clean up your damn room!"

"Please, Mommy. My room is already clean."

"Gotti, don't you lie to me. What I say?"

"It is, and I don't wanna stay here. It's boring."

"Go play in the backyard or downstairs, or something. All them damn video games you got around here to play with . . . go and do that. But don't go outside right now. It's too damn early for this shit!"

Gotti pouted. "You never let me have any fun!"

"Boy, you better leave from my fuckin' door and stay your ass inside until I get up. And stop waking me up. I had a late night," Layla shouted.

Gotti turned around and marched away from the bedroom door upset. He frowned and stomped his feet slowly against the floor. He stormed downstairs and hurried by Bonnie and Clyde, who were lounging in the great room, busied with their smartphones. They didn't pay their little brother any attention.

Most times, it was like Gotti was invisible to them. They were rich teenagers with good looks, doing teens things, including having sex.

Bonnie was texting her older boyfriend and planning to meet with him later in the day. Clyde was chatting with friends and looking at porn.

Gotti went outside to join his friends, who had already retrieved their bikes. "Let's go!" he said to them.

"Your moms say it was cool?" Reggie asked.

"No. But I'm going anyway." He knew his mother would most likely be sleeping all afternoon.

Reggie shrugged.

"I know where we can go," Duane said.

Gotti went to remove his mountain bike from the four-car garage and climbed on it. He popped a wheelie in the yard for fun, showing off his skills. Defying his mother's command, he followed behind Reggie and Duane, away from the sprawling property and into the neighborhood. Kids—horsing around and being kids.

Wacka sat in a stolen blue Hyundai and smoked his cigarette. He had his goons watching the house in a minivan decorated like a cable van, parked nearby. Wacka watched three boys on bikes exit the gated property. He couldn't believe his luck. Nine-year-old Gotti was leaving the premises with his friends. Wacka knew it was him, from the pictures Max had mailed him.

Gotti pedaled feverishly with his friends and soon passed the cable van and the Hyundai.

Wacka extinguished his cigarette, put the car in drive, and made a quick U-turn. He followed behind Gotti and his friends. The kids were moving steadily and having their fun. Wacka drove at a moderate speed a few clicks behind the boys. He was waiting for the right moment to strike.

The area was posh and quiet, and the driveways were long. Each home was worth a million dollars or more. There wasn't a noticeable police presence, and traffic was light on the streets.

Soon they'd ridden three miles from his home. The boys were on a long, isolated stretch of road that traveled several miles. The road cut right through the swampy wilderness.

Gotti pedaled zealously, leaving his friends behind and moving in the distance. He worked the mountain bike adeptly and did another wheelie in the middle of the street. Wacka eyed Gotti from the car, ready to make his move.

The Hyundai sped up behind him. Gotti heard the car and glanced back, but he didn't see it as a threat. He figured it would pass him by.

Wacka pushed his foot on the gas, and the car accelerated to 60 mph. He had Gotti dead in his sights.

Gotti continuously glanced back at the car, which was coming at him fast. He got nervous. He pedaled faster and felt the urge to look for safety, but on the remote road, there was nowhere safe.

The Hyundai reached 70 mph, and Gotti tried to swerve out of the way, but Wacka turned sharply toward the boy and mowed him down in broad daylight. The impact lifted Gotti and his bicycle at least twenty feet into the air, and he came crashing down on the concrete violently, his bike broken and twisted from the impact.

Wacka kept moving, speeding away from the scene. He left the boy dead on the road for his friends to find.

Wacka met up with his two goons in the van. He ditched the Hyundai somewhere remote, set the car on fire, and watched it burn for a moment. The heat was intense, and the fire quickly engulfed the entire car. He climbed into the van and left.

Gotti's friends were shocked. Their friend was dead. They didn't know what to do. They panicked, with Reggie screaming, "He's dead! He's dead!"

They were frightened kids in shock. They hurried away from the body in pure terror and rushed back home, scared to tell anyone what happened to their friend.

Reggie and Duane felt they had done something wrong because Mrs. Layla told Gotti not to leave the house, but he did it anyway. They were scared they would get blamed for everything.

Half the day went by, and Layla was still asleep in her bedroom. Bonnie and Clyde were off doing their own thing, and the house was extra quiet. She awakened a little after four p.m., and the first thing she did was light a blunt and step out onto the balcony to get some air. The sun shined brightly, and her property looked like a ghost town. The quietness was needed.

She went back into her bedroom and picked up her cell phone. She had several missed calls. She would call them back later. She thought about Lucky, Meyer, and Bugsy. The last time she'd heard from them, they were in Delaware. Scott had her babies away from New York. She wasn't too worried about them, since they knew how to handle themselves. Besides, they were protected. Their organization was a large machine with many moving parts. While Scott and the older children were handling business up north, she was taking care of business in the south, securing her family's longevity.

Layla finished her blunt and relaxed in her bedroom. She needed a drink and some good gossip. She poured herself some white wine and called a few friends to talk.

Two hours went by, and the house was still quiet. It was getting late, and yet, no Gotti. She walked around the house, which was vast and easy to get lost in, but no one was home, not even Bonnie and Clyde. She called Gotti's cell phone, but there was no answer. She moved through the house calling out her son's name, but nothing.

In Gotti's bedroom were the remnants of his two friends sleeping over the night before. There was trash and junk food left on the floor, toys and video games spread out everywhere, his bed was unmade, and his clothes were piled messily in the corner. The place was a pigsty. Gotti had lied to her. Layla was ready to curse his ass out and beat him.

She went into the front room and saw Bonnie was coming through the front door. The first thing out of Layla's mouth was, "Have you seen your little brother?"

"I haven't seen him all day," Bonnie said.

Layla sighed. She tried not to worry. He was probably somewhere upset and hiding from her because she wouldn't allow him to go bike-riding with his friends. She called his cell phone again but soon heard it ringing inside the house. She found it in the great room, near his video games. She worried that he didn't have his phone with him.

"Where's Clyde?" Layla asked.

Bonnie shrugged. "I don't know."

"Y'all fuckin' kids are gonna give me a fuckin' heart attack!" She got on her phone and dialed Clyde's phone.

"What, Ma?"

"Have you seen your brother?"

"No, I don't know where Gotti's at. He's not home?"

"If he was home, would I be fuckin' asking you?"

"He got friends, right? They spent the night, so why don't you call them? He probably over one of their houses."

Layla knew something was wrong. She felt it in the pit of her stomach. The last time she heard from her son was late in the morning. After sleeping most of the day and spending another two hours talking on her phone, she had no idea how long he'd been gone. *Why didn't I check on him sooner?* Layla cursed herself.

She did what Clyde suggested and called his two friends, but neither boy picked up the phone.

Bonnie lounged in the house like she gave no fuck that her brother was missing. It made Layla upset, and she cursed Bonnie out. She moved around in a panic. She tried not to break down in tears. She had to remain strong, believing Gotti would return home soon. He was stubborn. He wanted to have his way, and he wanted to scare his mother. It was working.

"I gotta call Scott," Layla said.

"You need to call the police," Bonnie suggested, now worried about Gotti.

Layla and Scott were raised to never involve cops. If there was an issue, then they learned to handle it on their own. She was born a gangster. But this was her son missing—her baby boy, her youngest—and that street code of ethics went out the door. Layla had to do what she needed to do. Scott was in New York, and she felt lost. She called 911 and reported her son missing.

Hours went by and still no Gotti.

Clyde came home, anxious about his missing baby brother.

Layla's panic turned into full-blown fear. She couldn't help but fear the worst. She needed to call Scott and tell him the bad news.

When Scott answered his phone, she said in one breath, "Gotti's missing. You need to bring your ass to Florida now. You need to find him!" Her voice trembled with distress and worry.

Scott couldn't believe what he was hearing. There was no way his son was missing. "I'm on my way there," he said.

Moments after she hung up, there was firm knocking on the front door. Gotti had his own key, but wishful thinking made her believe he'd lost it.

Layla approached the door with butterflies in her stomach. She felt an uneasy feeling swoop through her. When she opened the door and saw two uniformed cops standing right in front of her, she knew it was bad news. Before they could open their mouths, Layla broke down in tears.

"Mrs. West?" one cop asked.

"Please . . . no. Please, don't tell me—" Layla felt her knees weakening. She had to hold onto the doorframe for support.

Bonnie and Clyde stood right behind her. They too could feel the tension.

"Ma'am, we're sorry to inform you, but your son was the victim of a hit-and-run. He didn't make it."

Layla collapsed in anguish and released a bone-chilling scream that seemed to echo forever, her face swallowed by tears and torture. Her body gave out on her, and she was on the floor, feeling stuck there.

The two officers gave their condolences, but there was nothing they could say or do to alleviate her pain.

Bonnie and Clyde were crying too. Clyde had to console his mother. Bonnie couldn't believe it. Suddenly, their perfect life wasn't perfect.

Gotti had been found that afternoon several miles from the house, dead and alone with no ID. It was through the missing person's report that they'd found Layla to notify her of her son's death.

1995

Maxine's time on Rikers Island made her feel like Alice in Wonderland, going deeper and deeper down the rabbit hole. But this land was treacherous and a lot scarier. She had no friends, and although her crime was murder, she had no fearsome reputation to fall back on. She felt like a sheep in the wolves' den. She tried not to cry, but it was hard to hold back the tears. She'd received twenty-five years. She couldn't comprehend doing that many years in prison. She knew she would not make it.

Maxine's first eight months in Rikers were rough. She had a high-profile case, so it was no secret she was in there for murdering a pregnant woman. The inmates called her a "baby killer." It made her feel a lot worse.

Because she was pretty, some girls took a liking to her. She had a few confrontations and skirmishes inside Rikers Island, but nothing where she was scarred for life or beaten so badly she needed medical attention. Maxine was adjusting to her new life of confinement, but every day was a battle. Every day she lost a piece of who she was. Her dream of being a law school student was forever gone.

She befriended a girl inside named Key. Key was from the Bronx, and she had a baby face, but a sketchy reputation. She was connected to some hardcore and dangerous people. When Key found out Maxine was once a law student, she asked for help with her case. Skeptical of everyone inside the jail, Maxine didn't want to help her out at first, but over time, they talked and got to know each other. Bit by bit, Maxine helped Key out with her case.

Key was caught with a few eight balls of cocaine during a search of her vehicle during a routine traffic stop. Maxine felt that with her lawyer's help, they might shave some years off her sentence because of a technicality Maxine came across. Key appreciated the advice and the time. Hanging out with Key gave Maxine some leeway with the other inmates, and they gave her the nickname "Bookworm" in Rikers.

For the first seven to eight months, Scottie came to visit Maxine on Rikers Island. She was soon to be transferred to Bedford Hills Correctional Facility for Women in upstate New York. For the time being, Maxine was grateful that Scottie was visiting her. It meant he still loved her. He still cared. But then, as the date of her transfer upstate neared, she noticed his distance.

A week before her transfer, Maxine entered the visiting room in her gray jumpsuit and her long hair in a plain ponytail. Her face was always sad. Although she had been on Rikers Island for months, she could never get used to the place.

Scottie sat at a table, chilling. Maxine went to him, but he didn't get up to give her a hug or kiss. He just sat there, looking nonchalant. His aloof demeanor bothered Maxine, but she didn't make a big deal about it.

She sat opposite of him and said, "It's good to see you, Scottie." She smiled, but he didn't smile back.

"How you holding up?"

"I'm still trying, Scottie. I hate this place. They're transferring me upstate next week. I'm so scared."

"Just chill, Maxine. You'll be okay."

A combination of anger, sadness, and fear bubbled inside her. "I believed you, Scottie. You said I would be okay, but look at me now. Look at where I'm at. I swear, I should have just given them Layla, and I wouldn't be in this mess."

"You need to stop with this fairytale in your head, Maxine. If you had given up Layla, then what? You think the cops would have given you a get-out-of-jail-free card? You thinkin' delusional."

"It would have been a start to something."

"Sandy's purse was stolen, Maxine. Did you forget? You were there, and if you gave up Layla, then you would have been charged with felony murder instead of intentional homicide. The jury looked at you as you having the motive to go after Sandy, not Layla. You let Layla influence you, Maxine. You should have just stayed your ass home and waited for me to come and handle the situation. I would have handled Sandy."

Maxine shook her head from side to side in disbelief.

"I gave you everything, Maxine—a car, jewelry, clothes, and an engagement ring—and you had to fuck it up. You wanted to be this ghetto bitch and go to the projects and start some shit wit' Sandy. If I wanted a ghetto bitch, then I would have wifed Sandy, not you. You were my good girl, the one in school doing her thing, making something happen for herself. You let me down, Maxine. Did you let Layla influence you? Did you let that bitch get in your head?"

Maxine was stunned. After his speech, she wanted to leave. Things had gotten dry between them. They didn't hold hands across the table, and he could barely look at her, like he was hiding something. Or maybe he was ashamed of her.

Their visit ended with the CO's announcement, and Maxine was escorted back into lockup with several other inmates. She didn't want to look back at Scottie, but she did. He sat there for a moment, not even looking her way. As she was leaving the visiting room, she couldn't shake the feeling that this would be his last visit.

Maxine went back to her small cell feeling something was wrong, but she couldn't put her finger on it. She felt sick. She dropped to her knees and floated her face over the toilet. She threw up chunks and did a few dry heaves afterward.

She started crying again. Maybe Scottie was right. Had she given Layla up, her best friend would be doing jail time too. Plus, to be labeled a snitch in prison wouldn't have done her any good. And what good would it have done for them both to be incarcerated? Layla probably could help her out more by being free.

Her mind went back to meekness and vulnerability again. She also felt terrible for Scottie. He'd paid so much money for her attorney. He had big plans for her to become a lawyer, so he could brag to his friends that his girl was going to be the best defense attorney in the city. Now, look at her—a convict!

Meyer sat back on the bed relaxing as the cute girl with slim curves and full lips worked his hard flesh. Her lips moved up and down nice and slow, putting him into absolute bliss. His dick made her mouth stretch wide like a rubber band. He took a fistful of her long hair, grasped the back of the head, and made her deep-throat him. She didn't gag with eight inches disappearing down her throat.

Meyer closed his eyes and groaned, "Oh shit, ma! Keep doing that shit. I love it."

The young whore smiled and continued working her lips against his swollen member.

He was making the best of Delaware by finding pretty young girls to have his way with. It was something to do while the organization steadily progressed. He and Bugsy were making moves in Wilmington. They had enough muscle to build a wall around them and to wipe out any competition in the city. But things had to be subtle—no public bloodshed, no unnecessary violence unless it couldn't be avoided. They had to make bodies disappear out of town to make it look like a rival crew had killed a DMC member. Delaware couldn't be turned into a war zone.

Meyer hated the sneaking around in the dark. They were bigger than that. They were a powerful organization with millions of dollars and over a thousand soldiers spread across the country. His father's team was a force to be reckoned with. So why play careful with a bunch of nobodies? The solution was easy—put out a contract on Deuce. Take off the head, and watch the body fall. But there was one problem. Not too many people knew what Deuce looked like. He was smart enough to stay under the radar. Meyer felt that Delaware shouldn't be complicated to usurp. But it was.

Meyer felt the girl's sweet lips about to make him come. She did everything right. His worries had been substituted with pleasure. There was nothing like a good blowjob to keep the mind distracted. Still, his .45 pistol was within reach. He always kept his gun close.

Sudden knocking on the door made Meyer snapback to reality. He reached for his pistol. He made the girl pause her oral action and removed himself from the bed naked, the gun at his side.

"Meyer, open the door," he heard Bugsy say.

"Nigga, I'm busy."

"Yo, open the door. We need to talk. It's urgent. Pops called with some bad news," Bugsy said.

Meyer threw on a pair of jeans and unlocked the door. Bugsy stood there with his eyes watery. Luna stood behind him expressionless. Something was wrong.

"What is it?" Meyer asked. Bugsy's eyes never watered.

Bugsy stepped into the room and saw the naked girl on the bed. "She needs to leave."

Meyer didn't give it a second thought. He pointed his pistol at the girl and said, "Bitch, you heard what my brother said. Leave!"

She was taken aback by the sudden hostility. She jumped from the bed, grabbed her things, and ran out the room.

With her finally gone, Bugsy stared sadly at his brother and said, "It's news from Florida. Gotti's dead."

"What? What the fuck you talking about? Our little brother is dead? How the fuck—how?" Meyer's eyes watered now too. He could feel grief whirling inside of him. It had to be a mistake. Gotti was only nine.

"It was a hit-and-run," Bugsy said.

"A hit-and-run?"

"We need to go to Florida."

Meyer sat at the foot of his bed in sadness. It'd been a year since he'd last seen his little brother and his mother.

They say thugs don't cry, but Meyer and Bugsy both became emotional.

Bugsy sat next to his brother and said, "We gonna find the driver, and he's gonna pay for what he did to our little brother."

"I want him," Meyer said.

Gotti's funeral was fit for a king. It was a sunny day, and hordes of mourners gathered in the Queens cemetery to pay their respects to Scott West's youngest son. The gravesite was flooded with flowers, wreaths, and pictures of the smiling, handsome boy. Gotti's body was transported from the church to the cemetery in a white horse-driven carriage, and during the committal, over two dozen white doves were released into the air. It was a marvel to see the birds dance around the sky together, representing the soul's final journey. They looked like angels in the air.

Layla stood by her son's burial site in a black Valentino dress and large shades covering her sad, misty eyes. Scott stood next to her in solemn silence, looking healthy and handsome in his black Armani suit. He was in great pain, though it wasn't palpable.

Meyer, Bugsy, and the other children stood near their parents, all sharply dressed and each holding a white rose. They stared at the coffin, still in shock and overcome with sadness. Bugsy did his best to console a teary-eyed Lucky.

Meyer frowned, his anger growing more and more. Someone had to pay for their loss. Gotti was a mere child. He wasn't supposed to die. Gotti was supposed to be protected.

"For dust thou art, and unto dust thou shalt return." The preacher stood over the casket, Bible in hand, dressed in a long, black-and-white clergy robe with an embroidered cross.

The final words in reference to her baby boy sent Layla wailing in uncontrollable grief. "No! No! No! Please, God, bring him back to me. No!!" She wanted to wrap her arms around the casket and be entombed with Gotti. She dropped to her knees, her eyes saturated with tears. The pain was unbearable.

Scott stood still like a statue, his eyes fixed on the casket. One of his henchmen had to console his wife and lift her to her feet.

The siblings walked closer and each tossed their white rose on top of the casket.

Meyer had seen enough. Once he threw his rose and said his goodbye, he distanced himself from the ceremony, which was cluttered with gangsters, crime bosses, his father's business associates, and even a politician or two. He wanted to be alone. He smoked a cigarette in the distance.

While Meyer smoked in solitude, Scott was holding an impromptu conference with a few trusted lieutenants nearby. He was flanked by Whistler. "I want this muthafucka found," Scott snarled. "This is my son in the ground . . . my fuckin' boy!"

"I got peoples on it already," Whistler said.

"What do we know about the car?"

"Local police found a torched car on the same day. They believe it's connected to the crime," Whistler said.

"I need to know if this was deliberate or some scared fool trying to cover their tracks. I just want this murderer in my grasp by week's end," Scott said.

"We'll get our hands on any surveillance footage in the area, and we'll find a face," one of his lieutenants said.

"I want more than a face, I want a name," Scott said.

The man nodded.

Scott was in heavy mourning, but he composed himself. Who would have the audacity to go after his son? It was imperative he found the driver and questioned him before his demise. Was it a lone act, or was someone coming after his family? In his line of business, one never knew. He had to be sure, since he had enemies. Scott wanted to kill the man himself with his bare hands.

He turned to Whistler. "Make arrangements for my trip to Florida. I want the entire police report on my son's death. I don't want anything left out. And I want to meet the detectives handling the case. It's been a while since we've been down there thick. We need to make our presence known."

Whistler nodded.

Scott dismissed his lieutenants and went to rejoin his family. His son was already laid to rest, and his gold casket was ready to be entombed in the mausoleum. He only looked at Layla, having no words for his wife right now. His deadpan demeanor continued.

Meyer noticed his father's quick meeting with his lieutenants from where he stood, and it bothered him he wasn't involved. He had an idea what they were discussing. He wanted to avenge his little brother's death too. He had done everything his father had told him to do from jump, so there was no way he would miss an opportunity to exact revenge for his family's grief. He would put Delaware on hold and go down to Florida to comfort his family and handle the situation himself. He would argue against his father if needed. Though he was a hardcore gangster, Meyer had much love for his family. And if you fucked with them, then you fucked with him.

Meyer flicked away his cigarette and exited the cemetery. His mind was too dark with things, and he needed to leave. Being back in New York, he knew the right place to go to for a drink and some pussy. His strip club in the Bronx.

At the strip club, Meyer threw back a few shots of hard liquor and reconnected with a few friends and females. It felt like old times, though he hadn't been away that long. Delaware was a much different environment than New York. It was a business there, but there was no place like home.

The news of his little brother had spread fast. Some folks were ready to earn some cool points with Meyer and his family, promising him they would keep their ear to the streets, and if they heard anything he would be the first to know. Although the tragedy happened in Florida, they believed someone would be talking about it somewhere.

Meyer went into his office and closed the door. Luna kept him company. Luna was his protection and his close friend.

Meyer put the Grey Goose bottle to his lips and took a large swig. He then collapsed in his chair and leaned back. He looked at Luna and said, "My father is gonna try and keep me away. Like I'm not good enough to help him find who killed Gotti. He had a meeting at the cemetery and kept me out the loop. What the fuck is that about?"

"Your pops just got a lot on his plate," Luna said.

"First he sends us to Delaware to handle business, and me and Bugsy been doing that. Now he's holding court without us. I'm his son, and he's treating me like an outcast." Meyer took another hefty swig of Goose.

"We need to just chill."

"Nigga, you and me don't *just chill*. We're killers. We done proved numerous times that we can handle our own, do for this organization, *and* take care of business. Pops actin' like we some off-brand niggas." He took another gulp.

"So, what you got planned?" Luna asked.

"I don't know yet, but I need to show my father something—show him how important I am to his organization. There's a lot of shade being thrown my way."

"Whatever it is, you know I got your back."

"You my nigga, Luna. For real."

Meyer almost finished the bottle. He looked at the security monitors and saw his club running smoothly. Business was good. The girls were naked and lively, and the men were drinking and having fun.

Meyer noticed Lollipop was missing from the scene. At a time like this, he needed to see her. Drinking had him hot and bothered. He looked for Lollipop on the monitors, but she wasn't there. "Where's Lollipop?"

"Don't know."

Meyer finished the bottle and tossed it. Now he was full of liquor and looking sour and moody. He continued to stare at the security monitors.

He saw Lollipop finally arrive at the club, and she wasn't alone. She'd come with Sergeant McAuliffe. He immediately jumped up from his chair, grabbed his pistol, and stormed out of his office.

Luna saw his rage and followed him out the room.

Meyer's eyes were bleeding red with conflict as he marched toward them, the gun gripped tightly by his side. *The disrespect.* He'd told her to stay away from the cop. The crowd between Meyer and the cop parted. Everyone knew not to get in his way. Meanwhile, Sergeant McAuliffe had his back turned to the threat.

When Lollipop saw Meyer coming, her eyes widened with shock and fear. She didn't think he would show up there.

"Hey, cop!" Meyer shouted at McAuliffe.

McAuliffe turned around, only to be struck in the face with the butt of the gun. Meyer hit him again, and the overweight cop went down. Five or six times the gun smashed into his face, spewing blood and crippling the officer.

Lollipop shrieked in fear.

"You fuck wit' me! You fuck wit' me, huh?" Meyer shouted. Suddenly, he glared at Lollipop, who stood frozen in fear. He trained the gun at her head. "I told you, bitch, stay away from this nigga!"

Luna was the only one crazy enough to stop Meyer. "Not here. Now is not the time." He stepped in and held Meyer back from killing them both. There were too many witnesses around. It would have been a stupid move, and McAuliffe was still a cop. "We need to leave."

Meyer was breathing hard, and feeling tense. Killing McAuliffe would have been a major release of stress. He gazed down at the cop, his face bloody and a few things looking broken. Meyer had done a number on him. McAuliffe couldn't even pick himself up off the floor. Scowling, Meyer thundered, "It's a new fuckin' day!" and he and Luna soon left.

Outside, Luna took out his cell phone and made a call. When Whistler answered, he quickly said, "Yeah, it's me, and we got a problem."

Standing beside the floor-to-ceiling windows in his Manhattan apartment, Whistler smoked his cigar and gazed at the lights dancing and sparkling in the night. Every night, the city was bustling with activity. New York wouldn't be New York if it didn't move like a well-oiled machine.

The earlier call from Luna was a disturbing one. Meyer had gone too far with Sergeant McAuliffe because he couldn't control his temper over some pussy. Whistler shook his head, taking a puff from the cigar. He knew Scott would be furious when he heard the news.

The soft knocking at Whistler's door made him change his focus. He had an idea who it was so late in the hour. Always cautious, he peered through the peephole and saw Lucky standing in the hallway. It hadn't been a full twenty-four hours since they'd laid Gotti to rest.

He opened the door, and she wrapped her arms around him desperately. "I don't wanna be alone tonight. I just want to be loved and held by you."

"You're alone, right?" he asked.

"Of course, I'm alone. Why wouldn't I be?"

Whistler glanced left and right into the hallway, making sure there was no unexpected company. Scott could have had goons following his daughter for her protection without her knowing it.

As soon as Whistler closed his door, Lucky continued to come at him sexually. The two kissed passionately, their bodies entwined.

Lucky looked enticing in a beaded trim minidress with a plunging neckline that highlighted her ample cleavage. Her young eighteen-year-old flesh was breathtaking. She reached for his zipper and slid her hand inside, grabbing a handful of dick. Whistler lifted her dress to her hips, only to find out she wasn't wearing any panties. They kissed and fondled each other while their bodies heated up with the urges of sexual gratification.

Lucky pulled away from him, breaking their sexual momentum. "I need to take a shower. It's been a long day." She peeled off her dress, dropped it on the floor, and kicked off her shoes. She walked to the bathroom.

Lucky nakedness was eye candy for an older man like Whistler. A stab of guilt hit him. There he was, putting his dick in his friend's little princess while his son was fresh in the tomb.

Whistler heard the shower turn on and sighed heavily. With problems surfacing for the organization, sex should have been the last thing on his mind. Especially with Lucky. But he was a gangster with needs. He pivoted toward the bathroom and started to undress.

Beneath the cascading warm water, Lucky straddled Whistler and rode his hardness. Sex with the eighteen-year-old wasn't right, but it felt good.

She came, and her entire body felt like it was about to burst with pleasure. Every inch of her felt sensitive. He grew harder inside her as she pulsated. It didn't take long for Whistler to release inside of her.

Meyer rode silently in the back seat of the black Yukon traveling east on the Long Island Expressway. The scenery went by speedily, with traffic being light. It was dusk. The sun was steadily falling behind the horizon and painting the sky different shades. The truck was so quiet, the men could hear a fly fart.

Luna sat by his friend's side. Both were armed and worried. The two men in the front seat were Scott's henchmen, simply doing a job they were told to do.

Meyer knew he'd fucked up with Sergeant McAuliffe. The liquor and emotions had gotten the best of him. He heard the cop had suffered a broken eye socket, a broken cheekbone, and a bruised face. Not to mention a bruised ego. Now Meyer was worried about the consequences from Scott.

The driver navigated his way into an affluent area called East Hills with lovely homes and quiet streets. The Yukon approached a park near a lake nestled in the neighborhood and stopped. Meyer and Luna got out.

Scott was standing alone near a park bench, smoking a cigar and looking pensive. Solitude sometimes was his strength. Meyer approached his father alone, while Luna stood back.

Scott, looking nonchalant, fixed his eyes on his son. Meyer knew when his father looked too cool, it was a serious problem.

The moment Meyer was close, Scott clenched his fist and swung at him, his knuckles crashing into the side of Meyer's face. The punch sent Meyer stumbling.

"You're a fuckin' imbecile!" Scott yelled, his face flaring up with rage.

"Can I explain?" Meyer blurted.

"Shut the fuck up! If it weren't for Bugsy being your twin, I wouldn't even think you were my damn son. You know what it's gonna take to fix this shit? Do you?"

Meyer had no answer. He frowned, locking eyes with his angry father, still feeling the effect of the punch.

"Lucky for you, Whistler took care of things. It cost us money and favors," Scott said. "I should have them lock you up for your foolishness. But I already have one son dead. I don't need another in jail. But you owe the organization everything, starting with a hundred thousand dollars. And you're demoted. You no longer run the club or move any of the organization's products. You are a man in purgatory, and if you keep fuckin' up, then you'll be a man without a country."

Meyer could only listen. He didn't expect so many repercussions. Losing the club and being fined a hundred thousand dollars was painful enough, but to be demoted was humiliating.

"Pop—"

"Shut up, and don't speak! You've lost your speaking privileges with me."

Scott was one of the few people that Meyer couldn't bully or intimidate. His father was the apex predator at the top of the food chain.

"And that bitch that has you possessed, she's fired from the club. No person should act that crazy over pussy unless he's married to it. Now get the fuck out of my face! I have nothing else to say to you," Scott growled.

Meyer turned and marched away, feeling defeated by his father's words. He felt he was his own man, but Scott wanted to make him feel like a little boy.

Scott remained in the park, smoking his cigar. If Meyer wasn't his son, then he would be expendable.

M ax stood watch at the foot of the prison cell and could hear the correction officer's grunts and moans. Behind her, one of her girls was getting fucked doggy-style in the cell by Officer Fleming, a tall country redneck. Fleming couldn't get enough of Pumpkin, a short, dark-skinned inmate with a juicy booty, who was doing ten years for armed robbery and assault. Pumpkin was bent over with her pants down, legs spread, and clutching the metal sink fastened to the brick wall.

Officer Fleming happily thrust his small penis in and out of her, and soon felt his orgasm brewing. For Pumpkin, it was another fuck, another dollar. She was addicted to heroin, and she needed it daily to move on with her day.

The top tier was quiet. Max stood stern faced, her head swiveling left and right, watching out for any unexpected company—guard or inmate. She wanted Fleming to finish. He was always quick—five minutes or less.

"I'm gonna come!" he announced.

Pumpkin stayed quiet, as always. And soon it was over. He released, and she got paid. For the sexual rendezvous, she earned fifty dollars.

Officer Fleming exited the cell tucking in his shirt, but a part of it was still un-tucked. He looked sexually gratified. He walked away like nothing happened. It was back to work.

Max went into the cell where Pumpkin was cleaning up between her legs. She looked unbothered by the encounter.

Pumpkin held up the used condom with her index finger and her thumb. The latex condom was weighed down with semen. "That muthafucka let off a huge load this time. Look at this shit, Max. It seems like he wanted to put a baby in me."

"Well, that can't happen," Max said. "Flush it."

Pumpkin dropped it into the toilet and flushed it away. She then got herself decent.

Max covertly passed Pumpkin the small parcel filled with heroin at a cheaper cost. Correction Officer Mark had successfully smuggled in another batch of contraband, and Max was making her rounds around the prison.

Pumpkin smiled. The parcel in her possession was like gold to her. She was ready to snort it. It was the only way for her to get high. Having a syringe inside the prison was just too risky.

"Be careful with that," Max told her, before walking away to deal with other business.

In the dayroom, Shiniquia was on the telephone. The moment she saw Max, she smiled and curtailed the phone call. She took a seat next to Max and said, "It's done. My brother did his thing, and that little muthafucka went down with a hard bang, just how you wanted it."

Max was pleased to hear the news.

"He's ready for more. The money's good," Shiniquia said.

Max nodded. "I'll make the call to the bitch and set up another payment arrangement."

"Cool. How stupid this bitch is! She paid for the hit on her own son. Damn, you really are a cold-hearted muthafucka, and you really hate this bitch. Max, you is on some wicked shit, fo' real. I know that bitch owes you, but remind me to never get on your bad side."

Max simply smiled. Vengeance was hers, and it would continue to be hers until every last member of the West family was dead.

Layla lazed and sipped on white wine in the large tub in her Manhattan suite. It was a balmy night with clear skies, but her forecast was a heavy heart. She wasn't in any rush to go back to Florida. Their estate in Key West would become a bad memory for her. It was still hard to believe that Gotti was dead. She wished she'd paid him more attention that day.

All of her projects had been put on hold. Taking care of business with a grieving heart was hard. She sighed heavily and soaked in the tub, trying to find some escape from her pain. Every day there was tears for Gotti. And every day there was regret and nostalgia.

The police believed the hit-and-run was an accident, and the driver of the car most likely got scared and took off. The area where Gotti was killed was isolated, and there weren't any witnesses to give the license plate number of the car or describe the driver. Gotti's friends weren't much help. They saw nothing.

Layla felt that someone had to pay. There was no way someone would get away with killing her son. The pain was much greater with that person still walking around free and still breathing. Even if she had to hit the streets herself and play detective, someone had to be held accountable for Gotti's death. She had enough money to extract information from whomever, and she'd put the word out—a quarter of a million dollars for any information connected to her boy's death.

The suite was dim and so quiet, Layla could hear her thoughts. Soon she heard movement in the other room. Cautiously, she removed herself from the tub, toweled off swiftly, and put on a long robe. She then reached for the .38 on the bathroom sink. The family was known for keeping guns around at close range. It was a habit.

She exited the bathroom and stepped into the adjacent room with the loaded gun. She stepped into the huge furnished living room, ready for anything. To her surprise, it was Scott. He stood by the minibar pouring himself a drink. He looked her way, and there was no friendly acknowledgment. It almost looked like he carried some disdain toward his wife and mother of his kids.

Scott downed the vodka. He looked at his wife and said, "I'm flying to Florida tomorrow. I need to handle some business."

"Are you looking for the muthafucka that killed our son?"

"What you think I'm going to Florida for? To catch a tan? I got my peoples already on it." He poured himself another shot of vodka and tossed it back.

"You find him, baby, and you take care of that muthafucka. You make them pay fo' what they did to our family."

Scott poured another drink and threw it back.

"Are you staying the night?" she asked him.

"I have someplace else to be."

"Like where?"

"Don't question me. I got too much going on right now for you to start acting this way. Now is not the time, Layla."

"When will it be the time, Scott?" She looked at him with eagerness and then sadness. It'd been nearly two months since they'd had sex. And tonight, she needed him around. She wanted to be held and talked to. She wanted to be loved and fucked. She didn't want to be alone.

"When was the last time you took me into your arms and held me, Scott? When was the last time you fucked me? I'm aching and grieving here, and you ignore me. I'm still your wife, and I still love you. I just want us to be together."

Scott paused for a moment before pouring yet another shot.

Layla moved toward him. "Do you blame me for Gotti's death? Huh? You think it's my fault? Yeah, I shoulda been watching him, but I need a life too. I have a life, and it was supposed to be wit' my husband. I'm lonely here, Scott. I need you!"

Scott threw back his drink. "I need to go."

"So that's it? You need to go. Why did you come here in the first place?"

Scott put the glass on the counter and exited the room. Layla marched behind him, desperate for his attention. She grabbed his right arm, and he spun around with aggravation and jerked himself from her grip.

"Get off me, woman! I don't have the time to deal with your pettiness. I got things to do."

The look in Scott's eyes was intense. He looked like he was ready to strike her.

Tears trickled down Layla's face. "Who is she?"

"Don't question me, Layla. Look at your life. Look at how you live, flamboyant and on top. Why? Because of me. I provided you this type of life. I made you, and I can break you. So stay the fuck out my business!" He turned and marched out the door.

Crippled with a throbbing sorrow that felt never-ending, Layla dropped to her knees in heartache. She didn't want to be alone tonight, but there was no one to hold her and comfort her. There was luxury and gold, but no love, no affection, and no sex. This wasn't exactly the fairytale life she had envisioned for herself.

Scott sat in the back seat of the shiny black Escalade parked near the shoreline and smoked his cigar with several armed goons close by. The area was quiet and regulated with Scott's people, so there was no unwanted company.

Florida's heat was stifling. Even with dusk settling over the city, it still felt like it was a hundred degrees. Dressed sharply in a three-piece suit, looking like a mafia don with his gold cufflinks and pricey watch, he grieved his son's death in his own way. Keeping busy was one way. Another way was infidelity.

But this thing with his son bothered him. Something wasn't right, and he wanted to get to the bottom of it. What type of person ran down a child and fled the scene? Scott didn't care if the driver turned out to be a sixteen year old kid; anyone connected to his son's death would die slowly.

He puffed on his cigar as he gazed at the calm ocean. It seemed like a gateway, with the fresh waters peeking at the dry earth above. Occasionally the sea gently rolled against the soft sand and moved back to its watery home, as the sunset cast an evening light against the shore.

Soon, another vehicle approached. The bright headlights belonged to a white Escalade, which parked in front of Scott's car. The rear doors opened, and two men climbed out. One was a detective named Joseph Mastery.

Before meeting with Mastery, Scott researched everything about him. He had fifteen years on the police force, eight years with Miami-Dade, and then he became a homicide detective in Key West. He had been married to his beautiful wife Jennifer for five years, and they had one boy and two girls. His parents were still living. His police record was okay—a few little bumps here and there, but nothing too wild. His personal life seemed ordinary, minus his gambling habit. He was in debt for ten thousand dollars to a local bookie.

Scott's men went to Mastery's home to collect him for a meeting. It wasn't a choice. Detective Mastery seemed alarmed by their sudden presence, but he complied. He told his wife he'd be right back and left with the men. The men told him there would be no need for his firearm.

One of Scott's men escorted him to the black Escalade. He approached the window and asked Scott, "You ready to see him, boss?"

Scott nodded.

The passenger door opened, and Mastery was told to get into the truck. He got in and sat next to Scott.

"Why am I here?" Mastery asked.

Scott puffed his cigar and didn't speak for a beat. He wanted the cop to feel his power. "You know my son?"

"Pardon me?"

"You're the detective investigating his death, and I want the case file on my son's murder."

"I can't," the detective said.

"In my world, there's no such thing as *can't*. When I want something done, or if something is needed, I'll get it either way, Detective. Now, I want the file, and I want information on the case. And before you continue to contest me, I hope you'll consider that there can either be retribution or reward." Scott dropped a thick manila envelope filled with cash onto the detective's lap. "There's twenty thousand dollars there, enough to pay off your gambling debts and still treat your family to something really nice."

Joseph Mastery picked up the envelope and stole a look inside. He was shocked to see only hundred-dollar bills clustered together, definitely a lot of money in his eyes. "Whoa!"

"Now, can we talk?"

Mastery exhaled. "What do you need to know?"

"Tomorrow, I want everything you have in my possession," Scott said.

Mastery nodded.

Scott took another draw from the cigar and exhaled. The back seat clouded with smoke, but Mastery wasn't bothered by it.

"Gotti meant the world to me, Detective, and his life was stolen from him."

"My condolences. I'm a father myself. I can only imagine."

"What do I need to know right now about the hit-and-run?"

Mastery paused for a beat. He sighed. "First, I don't believe it was an accident. Where your son was struck, there weren't any skid marks to indicate the driver intended to brake or stop. And from the forensics deposition, the car had to be traveling a good speed, say maybe sixty to seventy miles per hour."

"So it was a murder?"

"Unfortunately, yes."

Scott fumed on the inside.

The detective added, "We found the car torched right after. It had been reported stolen. The owners of the vehicle are law-abiding and taxpaying citizens; nothing strikes me as suspicious about them. Their alibi checks out."

"And the driver of the car?" Scott asked.

"Nothing yet. The fire destroyed any evidence that might have been inside the car. We don't have a face or name. But a few witnesses saw a cable van in the area around the time of the incident with your son."

"You've done your job well, Detective. Thank you. I expect the file tomorrow," Scott said coolly. "That's all."

Mastery nodded.

The rear passenger door opened, and one of Scott's goons was waiting to escort Detective Mastery back to his home. Mastery climbed out of the SUV and walked back to the vehicle he'd arrived in.

Scott sat wordlessly in the back seat, consumed by his thirst for vengeance. He didn't want the cops to find Gotti's killer. He wanted to locate the man himself and make him beg for death.

T hree weeks after her son's funeral, Layla flew back to Florida first class on American Airlines. Though she was reluctant to leave New York and wanted to be close to her son's gravesite, she still had business in Florida to take care of. The moment she announced to Scott she was heading back to Florida, he was ready to return to New York.

Bonnie and Clyde had the courage to go back earlier and had the estate to themselves. Scott had booked the Four Seasons Hotel so that he could freely hold meetings with the underworld in an attempt to locate his son's killer. He needed to keep Bonnie and Clyde away from the family business until things settled down. They took full advantage of not being chaperoned by their mother or father. Housekeepers, a driver, gardeners, and credit cards helped them maintain, but neither parent was around full-time anyway. They missed Gotti, but their lives went on. New York was a happening place, but the twins enjoyed Florida more with its warm weather, beaches, and upbeat atmosphere. They couldn't wait to move there full-time.

The black Maybach pulled into the circular driveway and stopped at the front entrance of the home with the two large pillars. The chauffeur climbed out and opened the back door for his passenger.

Layla swung her legs around, and her "red bottoms" touched the pavement to her property. She climbed out of the sleek Maybach, looking stunning in a short sundress and big hat. She took a deep breath and stalled. She had a quick flashback of the two cops showing up to her door to deliver the bad news.

"I'll get your things, Mrs. West," the chauffeur said.

Layla nodded. She climbed the stairs to the entrance, and the wide front doors opened on cue. Bonnie and Clyde greeted their mother with smiles on their faces.

Layla hugged her children and went inside. Everything was the way she'd left it. The staff had taken good care of the place. "I need a drink," Layla said.

The maid hurried off to fulfill her request. She soon returned with a Daiquiri made with rum, simple syrup, and lime juice.

Layla wasted no time drinking it. On the way to her bedroom, she stopped at Gotti's bedroom and peeked inside. It was the same—messy and undisturbed. His video games on the floor were a sad thing to her. He loved his video games. Layla wiped the tears from her eyes. She felt it was a mistake to look into the room so soon. She closed his door, releasing a deep sigh.

She went into her bedroom and closed the door. She needed a timeout. Everything felt so different. She took comfort on her bed, smoked weed, and ignored her phone calls. Tomorrow she would regroup and get back to business. Three weeks was a long enough hiatus.

The next morning, Layla sunbathed on the balcony naked like usual. It was another sunny and scorching day in the Sunshine State. With the kids gone and the staff off, she was able to enjoy the quiet. Solitude was something she'd gotten used to, especially with Scott continuously gone. She was looking forward to the landscapers coming by to treat and cut her yard. Fabian was always a treat to see. The more she saw him, the more she desired him.

She put a cigarette to her lips and inhaled the nicotine. Her pain was still raw, but she was getting by, doing everything in her power to hold it together.

Her cell phone rang. When she saw the number, she mustered up the courage to answer. It was a collect call from Maxine.

Something suddenly came over Layla when she heard Maxine's voice on the other end. She cried like a baby as she told her longtime friend about Gotti.

Maxine feigned shock over the phone and pretended to sob. "Ohmygod, Layla! My condolences to you. I'm so sorry for your loss."

Layla told her the story, and Maxine listened, although she knew the details already. But it was fun to hear it from Layla's mouth. Maxine took pleasure in Layla's grief. Yet, she was so believable about feeling her friend's pain, Layla tried to console her. It sounded like Maxine was taking the situation hard.

Then Layla started boasting about the funeral. "His funeral was spectacular, though. We sent our son out like a king. His casket alone was 'bout thirty thousand dollars, and we buried him in this Jewish cemetery in Queens. We had over a dozen doves fly into the air. In total, we spent over a hundred thousand dollars to send him off correctly. And so many important people came to pay their respects. He was laid to rest in his very own mausoleum, complete with a private sitting area inside, just like the great John Gotti."

Max was upset that Layla found a silver lining in her son's death. She wasn't grieving enough.

Maxine sighed. "Listen, I hate to bring this up, especially at a time like this, but I'm gonna need another favor from you. I need another thirty thousand sent to the same location."

"What? Are you serious?"

"I'm willing to work something out with the girl, but—"

"Shit, Maxine! You need to stand up for yourself and handle your muthafuckin' business. I can't always have your back and pay your punk dues. And you ask me now? Wit' Gotti dead? Fuck you, bitch!" She hung up, annoyed by Maxine's audacity.

That afternoon, Layla watched Fabian tend to her front yard, her needs screaming at her. Maxine had irked her nerves; she was highly irritated and watching the help was a distraction. Fabian's sweaty shirt was clinging to his deep muscles. Layla was completely transfixed by him. She stood against the balcony railing, admiring his biceps as they flexed with every movement of his arms.

They locked eyes. She smiled. He smiled.

Only his smile wasn't enough to free her mind from the pain and loneliness of losing her son.

Then, thoughts of Maxine invaded Layla's fantasy again. She hated herself for hanging up on her friend in her time of need. Layla was surprised Maxine had lasted twenty years in prison and she hadn't committed suicide or wasn't stabbed. Maxine could have easily given her up to save herself, but she kept her mouth shut all this time. Maxine really was a diehard friend.

Layla picked up her cell phone and made a call. "I need another certified check . . . thirty thousand dollars."

1995

Maxine felt like she was in a different world after she was transferred to Bedford Hills Correctional Facility for Women in Westchester County. Several hours from New York City, it was maximum security and the largest female prison in the state. Though she'd spent almost a year on Rikers Island, she once again felt like fresh fish in Bedford. It took some time for her to adjust to the big leagues. There were new guards, new rules, and the same danger, but from new inmates.

Questions peppered her mind. Who would come see her way up there? Her parents had their lives to live, and she didn't want them to focus solely on her troubles. She had cost them so much grief. And what was going on with her appeal? She needed to talk to her lawyer, yet when she called he was never in the office. The irony was that it was times like these that she needed Layla—the very person responsible for this mess. The one person, other than Scottie, that she wished would visit her. But neither came.

She figured Scottie was sticking his dick in some new bitch by now. She wasn't a fool. Truth be told, he was never faithful to her. Scottie had taken her virginity and was the only man ever inside her. Now there wouldn't be others, since there would be no love and affection from a man where she was.

Her first week at Bedford, several inmates tried her, but the guards intervened. Maxine was becoming hardened by the conflict and the prison itself and was gradually changing into someone she hardly recognized. Her first year of incarceration was the hardest, and then she learned to do the time instead of letting the time do her. She was learning the hard way but learning all the same.

Leanne befriended Maxine in Bedford. Leanne was Maxine's senior by ten years, but they had a few things in common. They'd both attended Catholic schools, come from homes with two parents, and had fallen in love with drug dealers. Now they were both doing hard time for murder after refusing to snitch.

Leanne was from Harlem and doing life for murder and conspiracy. She was part of a drug organization called GMN (Get Money Niggas) that netted thirty million dollars a year. GMN was notorious for extreme violence and intimidation, and Leanne was the first lady of the drug empire.

Tipped off by a mole in her organization, the authorities busted Leanne with five kilos of cocaine in the trunk of her Mercedes. They later found out she had an existing warrant for murder. The DA promised her leniency if she testified against her violent drug crew, but she refused. When Leanne heard Maxine's story, she respected her for keeping her mouth shut.

Over time, Leanne taught Maxine many things, particularly how to smuggle drugs and corrupt guards. She took Maxine under her wing and schooled her about prison life. Association with Leanne meant respect from the other inmates, but it also came with a cost, and Maxine became Max. Her rite of passage came the day Leanne needed a favor from her.

"I need this bitch got," Leanne had said to her.

"Who?" Maxine asked.

"Sonia." Sonia and Leanne had a rivalry that started from the streets and continued in prison.

Though Maxine had been sentenced for murder, she'd never killed anyone in her life. But Leanne needed the favor done ASAP, and she trusted Maxine to carry out the deed. Leanne provided the murder weapon, which was a sharp shank made from a piece of material from the cot in their cells. The murder plot required the help of another inmate, Ginger, and a corrupt guard.

It took place near the showers early one morning. Sonia and her lesbian lover, Julie, were alone, having relations with each other in the shower. After their intimacy, Julie left the showers first to make her morning visit from family. Maxine approached the bathroom with Ginger, and the guard posted nearby stepped away for reasons unknown. Maxine waited for Sonia to exit. When she did, Maxine took a deep breath and they attacked. Ginger quickly subdued Sonia while Maxine plunged the shank into Sonia's back repeatedly. It was a daring feat, and one that made Maxine cringe, but it had to be done. She feared repercussions from Leanne if she didn't carry it out.

As Sonia lay dead on the floor, Maxine discarded the bloody shank. She and Ginger left Sonia's dead body for the guards to find.

After that, Maxine had Leanne's full trust and respect. Maxine was now Max, and her reputation was solidified.

After their uncomfortable visit before her transfer out of Rikers, Maxine wrote Scottie letter after letter without reply. She called his cell phone repeatedly, but then he changed his number.

Maxine's eyes were almost swollen shut from crying every night. At first, the inmates commiserated with her, understanding her pain. Each one of them had been betrayed by a man. But then Maxine had to suck it up.

Maxine received letters from Layla, but never a visit. Layla's excuse was she feared jail and prison and thought they would detain her and she would never be released. It was the same excuse Layla had for not attending Maxine's trial.

After a few months in Bedford, Layla sent a letter congratulating her for becoming an aunt to twin boys, Meyer and Bugsy. She didn't even know Layla was pregnant, and there was no mention of the twins' father. The letter was also accompanied by a large commissary deposit. *Guilty-conscience money*, Maxine thought. Layla had taken over where Scottie had left off. After she had blown trial it was just a matter of time before he had stopped dropping money off to her parents on her behalf. No visits, no letters, no money, and no Scottie.

During a casual phone conversation, Maxine's mother said she had seen Layla and Scottie together in the neighborhood. She assumed the two had become an item. It was heartbreaking news to Maxine.

Six weeks after the birth of her two sons, Layla wrote Maxine again, informing her about her sudden marriage. Her knight in shining armor was handsome, respected in the streets, and the father of her twin boys. But there was no mention of the groom's name, and no picture of him.

After Max had spent almost a decade in prison, Layla said to her one day, "Scott is taking me to Paris for our anniversary!"

It was that simple. From that day Layla would bring up Scott's name in her letters and in their phone conversations. It was bad enough that Layla's aggressive actions had taken Maxine's freedom, but now she had taken her man and flaunted the betrayal with letters of pregnancy, marriage, children, and wealth.

September 2014

Wacka sat at the bar drinking his beer and staring at the flat-screen TV perched over the bar. The Mets were losing to the Cubs by one point. The classy Downtown Brooklyn bar had just the right ambience for men to talk business over a few drinks, and for girlfriends to unwind, laugh, and flirt with a few suits. The décor was dark wood interior and high ceilings. It was early evening, and a few scattered patrons chitchatted amongst themselves, but the ballgame was louder.

A ruffian like Wacka was used to the hole-in-the-wall places with bullet holes, cheap drinks, and loose women, so The Breaker Bar on Fulton seemed out of his league. But he had his reasons for being there.

Wearing a white button-down and khakis, he'd disguised his real appearance. The demonic and gangland tattoos were covered with clothing, and his bald head was freshly shaved and gleaming like a bowling ball. He wore wire spectacles to soften his dark eyes, never mind the small pistol concealed in an ankle holster.

It was hard to tell he was a coldblooded killer—to deduce that he'd viciously mowed down a nine-year-old boy in the street. The news had gotten back to him about the boy's father, Scott West, and the murder contract put out on the street. It was a lot of money, but Wacka doubted anyone knew anything that could lead back to him. Wacka wasn't worried about consequences coming his way. The kill was clean. The car had been torched, no one had seen his face, and there wasn't anything incriminating left behind. And his peoples were loyal.

He downed his beer. "Bartender, let me get another one," he said.

The bartender nodded and went to get him a Bud Light.

It'd had been a slow day, but in a few hours, the nocturnal crowd would converge at the same bar, and it would look like an entirely different place with people, laughter, music, and beautiful women.

Wacka drank his next beer. New York was his town—big and busy with a lot going on, plenty of women everywhere, and easy to blend in and get lost among the crowds of people. He never had a problem getting business in the city. There was always somebody buying or selling something, even drugs.

The neatly dressed Caucasian man in a black suit and white tie that walked into the bar was slim and of average height. He was clean-shaven with dark black hair. He looked a Wall Street type. He immediately spotted Wacka at the bar.

Wacka turned slightly to see Fred Gilliam had finally arrived. He picked up his beer and a leather briefcase and greeted the white boy at a wall booth. They sat opposite each other and started their business.

"We okay?" Fred asked.

"Yeah, we good," Wacka replied.

"What's the damage for this load?"

"Thirty cents on the dollar."

"And that's two stocks, right?" Fred asked.

"Yeah, two pure stocks definitely up," Wacka said. Underneath the booth, Wacka slid the leather briefcase closer to Fred.

Fred carefully picked it up and looked inside. It was what he needed—two kilos. It was Christmas for him. His boys on Wall Street would make him a fortune like always. "I like it," he said.

"I know you would. It's why you were the first person I called."

A short waitress with an infectious smile soon came over and asked if they were interested in ordering drinks.

Wacka was already content with his beer. Fred ordered a whisky sour. She went to get Fred his drink.

Fred didn't care how Wacka got the product. It was his now, and he was getting it for a good price. He was already a wealthy man, being an adept stockbroker with the firm Saxon & Smith. Fred Gilliam had attained his Series 7 license when he was twenty-three years old, which was soon followed by his Series 63. He was notorious for his risk-taking and positive attitude, and he had the gift of gab.

But he had a wild, dangerous side. He grew up in Bensonhurst, Brooklyn and was connected to the mafia. He took up drug dealing to satisfy his taste for luxury items and an extravagant lifestyle.

He subtly handed Wacka a medium package containing thirty thousand dollars.

Wacka looked inside.

"We happy?" Fred asked him.

"Oh, we happy," Wacka said, smiling.

"It's always a pleasure doing business with you, my friend." Fred removed himself from the booth, buttoned his suit jacket, and walked away with the leather briefcase.

Wacka remained in the bar and finished his beer. He was a hustler, a drug dealer, a thief, and a contract killer prepared to make his money by any means necessary.

The waitress came to the table with Fred's drink but found him gone. "Did he leave?" she asked.

Wacka smiled at her attractiveness. He removed a knot of hundred-dollar bills and gave her a C-note.

She was shocked by his generosity. "Thank you."

"You're a beautiful woman. What time do you get off?"

Her smile continued. Wacka wasn't a bad-looking man. He carried an aggressive, bad-boy mannerism somewhat alluring to the ladies.

He handed her another C-note. "I can make it worth your time."

She continued to smile and took the cash.

Two hours later, the waitress's face was in Wacka's lap. Her head rapidly bobbed up and down in the front seat of his car, while Wacka reclined and enjoyed her skills. He cupped her small ass and fingered her tight vagina, stimulating her to some extent.

During the oral pleasure, his cell phone rang. It was Dagmar. He answered the call while his female friend continued to engulf him gratifyingly below.

"What up?" Wacka answered with ragged breathing, his voice barely above a whisper.

"Wack, you busy, nigga?"

"Kinda. What's up?"

"We on again. That payment was sent."

"A'ight, cool—Oh shit!"

"You fuckin' a bitch, nigga?"

"I'm doin' me, nigga," Wacka said. The waitress took all of him in a deep-throat, simultaneously cupping and massaging his balls.

"Tomorrow then," Dagmar said.

Wacka hung up and applied his full attention to the blowjob. "I wanna come in your mouth," he announced.

Bonnie stared at her image in the large mirror on her bedroom wall. She was ready for her first day of school, dressed in a short pleated skirt, white shirt, and green tie under a dark green blazer with her school's insignia on the breast. Her diamond tennis bracelet, diamond earrings, and diamond necklace—all gifts from her father—were worth close to a hundred thousand dollars.

She did a minor twirl in the mirror, checked out her backside, and smiled. "Smoking hot," she said to herself before yelling at Clyde to get a move on.

For Bonnie, school was more a fashion show than an education. She and Clyde were celebrities at the aristocratic academy school in Mount Vernon, New York. It was an exclusive and very expensive school for the privileged. And Bonnie and Clyde were very privileged. The boys loved Bonnie, and the girls were attracted to Clyde.

It was the first day of school, but this would be their last year of school in New York. This time next year she and Clyde would be living year-round in Florida and residing in the new lavish homes being built now. They couldn't wait for the twenty-four/seven sunshine, warmth, and sandy beaches. No more harsh winters, freezing cold, or wet snow. Bonnie wanted to be on the beach with her friends and showing off her bikini-clad body for Christmas and New Year's. Clyde wanted to swim in the ocean and flirt with the girls that flocked to him because of his playboy swag and muscles he'd gained from seeing his personal trainer three days a week. Handsome and tall with curly black hair, Clyde was becoming a heartthrob and a millionaire playboy at fifteen years old. Both siblings were already sexually active, Clyde more so than Bonnie.

Bonnie and Clyde left their Manhattan penthouse and descended to the main floor in the quiet elevator. The doors opened, and they stepped into the lobby with marble flooring and a stunning antique chandelier centerpiece in the atrium.

"Good morning," the front desk clerk greeted them.

Bonnie and Clyde ignored the man. They weren't keen on associating with the help.

Then they were greeted by Sammy the doorman in his Ritz-Carlton uniform. He nodded politely as he opened the glass doors and shepherded them through with a friendly attitude. "Have a wonderful and blessed day," he said.

They didn't tip him. He didn't mind.

Their chauffeur stood next to a black Maybach with the rear door already opened and ready for them to enter. There was a bodyguard for the twins, too—a tall, silent man in black looking threatening. Since Gotti's death, Scott wasn't taking any chances with his other children.

Bonnie and Clyde slid inside the vehicle, the chauffeur climbed behind the wheel, and the bodyguard rode shotgun. The twins were on their way to school, a forty-minute ride, depending on the traffic.

The vehicle traveled north on Park Avenue. The morning traffic was beginning, but it wasn't crippling. The twins were relaxed in the back seat, on their smartphones listening to music, playing games, and texting. The driver navigated the vehicle through East Harlem, where the local population was flooding the streets on their way to work or school.

Bonnie and Clyde didn't care for the area. They'd never been to Harlem, only passed through the urban neighborhood on the way to school. Not once did they gaze out the window and look at anything in the vicinity; their attention was consumed by their smartphones.

But the car caught people's attention. A Maybach driving through Harlem had to have someone important inside.

A red light brought the vehicle to a stop at the intersection of 123rd Street. A small crowd crossed the streets. The car idled next to a red Caravan on the driver's side, and adjacent to the traffic was the train trestle covering much of the street.

Unexpectedly, a dark Denali crashed into the Maybach, forcibly jerking the vehicle forward. The impact almost sent the car flying through the red light.

Bonnie and Clyde were tossed around the back seat. They were in shock.

"What the fuck!" The chauffeur quickly unfastened his seatbelt and removed himself from the car.

The bodyguard did the same, his pistol holstered. It appeared to be a fender-bender. Both men scowled at the minor accident.

"Can't you fuckin' drive, you idiot?" the chauffeur shouted.

The doors of the Denali opened, and two masked men emerged carrying Heckler & Koch MP7A1s. They aimed the deadly weapons at the chauffeur and bodyguard and opened fire before the bodyguard could unholster his gun.

Bratatatatatatatatatat!

The barrage of bullets created chaos. The gunmen killed the chauffer and bodyguard with a hail of gunfire, and their bullet-riddled bodies slumped against the street.

Bonnie shrieked. Clyde panicked. Through the windows of the Maybach, they witnessed the bloodshed of a working man and a hired goon. They were now alone. Tears welled in their eyes. There was nowhere for them to run.

The gunmen approached the car with their submachine guns aimed at the rear, ready to open fire.

"Ohmygod, Clyde!" Bonnie shouted in fear.

"Close your eyes, sis!" Clyde shouted. He tightly grabbed his sister in his arms and did his best to shield her from the danger.

Bratatatatatatatatatat!

Another barrage of bullets erupted into the car, shredding metal and then violently riddling the siblings with hot, sharp rounds. Their blood splashed all over the leather seats, and their bodies lay contorted against each other.

For good measure, one gunman opened the rear door to the car and fired at the bodies once more. Satisfied, they jumped into the idling Caravan and sped off, leaving a massacre behind. There was no longer a need for the Denali; it had served its purpose.

When the gunfire stopped, everyone was astounded by the daytime execution of four people.

Shortly after, dozens of police cars, uniformed cops, and homicide detectives flooded the intersection in Harlem. The entire area was cordoned off with yellow crime-scene tape, and the looky-loos came in droves to see the murders. They lingered behind the yellow tape wide-eyed at the gangland murder of four people. There were so many shell casings on the street that the detectives would lose count.

"Fuckin' Fallujah!" one detective commented about the gruesome crime scene.

The detectives stood around the Maybach, each sickened by the dead twins in the back seat, dressed appropriately in their uniforms. It was definitely overkill.

They discovered the dead bodyguard was armed with a Glock 19, which wouldn't have been much good against the submachine guns.

The witnesses couldn't describe the shooters. They wore masks and all black with colored bandanas. They left behind an SUV, which was surface clean and had no visible evidence. A tow truck had to take it back to the crime lab to dust for fingerprints, but it was doubtful. The vehicle had been reported stolen twenty-four hours prior.

For the moment, the only thing the NYPD could do was identify the bodies from their school IDs—Bonnie and Clyde West, children to businessman and alleged drug kingpin Scott West. The more they looked into the killings, the more it looked like a planned hit.

It was a nightmare. There was no way two more of her children were dead. Layla couldn't grasp it. She refused to accept the truth. The anguish crippled her like an electrocution chair. She had been strapped to it, and the volts hit her fiercely. She might as well die.

The loss of Bonnie and Clyde was a devastating blow to her. She locked herself in the bedroom in the dark and didn't want to be bothered by anyone. She cursed the staff and sobbed uncontrollably. It felt like the room was collapsing in on her, and there was no escape.

Someone was coming after her family. They were killing her children, and most likely, they wanted to kill her too.

When Scott received the news about Bonnie and Clyde, he nearly went through the roof with rage. How did they get to his kids? This wasn't a coincidence; this was an attack on his family. He called every lieutenant, soldier, and associate in his organization to an emergency meeting at one of his city properties. Everyone came armed, and everyone knew it would be a war, but with who? Though Scott was stricken with grief over the death of Bonnie and Clyde, he took charge of the assembly of his goons and clarified it—five million dollars for any information about anything, and another ten million dollars for the names of the people behind the attack. He wanted pain and death to ensue behind his kids' murders. He wanted total annihilation of the culprits, and he had the men, the resources, and the power to do so. But first he had to bring these foes from out of the dark.

"From now on, everything fuckin' stops, and y'all's only concerns are hunting the people responsible for the death of my children," Scott commanded.

They nodded, hungry to implement revenge.

"Twenty-four hours, seven days a week hunting and finding me information out there. I want faces and names. No one sleeps, no one eats. You treat this incident as the end of the fuckin' world!" he growled before dismissing them.

Scott's eyes were watery but still stern with anger and yearning for vengeance. He was ready to spread his wrath biblically—torch cities and wipe out generations if necessary.

Whistler stood by Scott's side. Being the friend and partner he was, he was grieving too, stunned by the boldness of the attacks on innocent kids. "I already made around-the-clock armed security arrangements for the rest of the family."

Scott nodded.

"What enemies do we have out there—past or present?" Whistler asked.

"In our business, many," Scott said.

"Delaware?"

"Possible," Scott said.

Could it have been Deuce? He was a local thug and a dangerous man, from the word on the streets. And supposedly smart too. But Scott felt that Deuce didn't have enough clout and information to get to his kids.

If Meyer and Bugsy did things correctly, then they should have been silent in their takeover of the area—no extreme or public violence.

Though skeptical, Scott put nothing past anyone.

"I think we have a snitch in our organization," Whistler said.

"I agree."

"For someone to get to Gotti in Florida—kill him like that—and now Bonnie and Clyde on their first day of school, I strongly feel it's an inside job."

"I want this muthafucka smoked out and brought to me, Whistler. You find this muthafucka quickly."

"I'll get Maze on it. He's good at infiltration, finding things and people that don't wanna be found."

"I'll pay him extra for this. And get in touch with my kids. Tell them what happened to Bonnie and Clyde and get Bugsy and Meyer back from Delaware. I need my children here where I can protect them."

Scott stood silent for a beat, his heart heavy and his mind boggled with trauma. He felt like he was about to go insane. "I want to be alone," he said to Whistler.

Whistler understood. He exited the room, giving his friend some time to grieve. He had never seen Scott in such a state. Though Scott appeared stable, Whistler knew the man was breaking down inside. Because of the manner in which Bonnie and Clyde were killed, Whistler feared more deaths and more agony. Whoever the enemy was, they were vicious and calculated, knowing who to strike and when. They came at Scott's core, his family, and were working their way through his family tree. First Gotti, and then Bonnie and Clyde. Who would be next?

Outside in the cold night air, Whistler removed his cell phone and called Lucky. His call went straight to voice mail. He was worried about her. His second call went to her voice mail again. He decided to go to her place to make sure she was okay. He climbed into his Range Rover and made haste to her apartment on the Upper West Side of Manhattan.

28

1999

Solitary confinement was degrading and could deteriorate an inmate's mind if she wasn't strong enough to survive the isolation. Max found herself inside the small, dark concrete room with no windows, naked and cold. The indignity was cruel, and she felt like a caged animal. But animals at the zoo, she felt, were treated better than this. She had spent sixty days in confinement with another thirty days to go. The punishment was harsh. She received her food and any other material through a rectangular slot in the steel door and barely had any human contact. There was no mail and no visitors. Three months was a long time to be alone, naked, and trying to keep your sanity. Her crime was fighting once again. She had put another inmate in the ICU.

"That bitch right there is stealin' from us, Max. This is the third straight week she's been short wit' the cash," Ginger had told Max.

Max had been moving drugs through the prison for several months. She supplied a few inmates for distribution and expected a sizable kickback. But an inmate named Rhea had been coming up short with payment lately. Rumor was, she had been bad-mouthing Max, trying to stir up some shit.

"She's playin' us," Ginger said.

Stealing from an inmate in prison was a sure sign of disrespect. Max knew she needed to teach Rhea a lesson—make an example out of her. If she didn't, then her other workers would try her too. Leanne had always told Max, "You let one get away with it, then you might as well let them all get away with it."

Max waited and watched. Then one day during lunch, Max was sitting with her cohorts in the cafeteria when she eyed Rhea coming her way. Rhea was calling her out indirectly without having to say a word. It was her movements, what she was doing, and what she was saying.

Max confronted Rhea. "You short bitch! Where's my fuckin' money?"

Rhea stood her ground. After a short, heated exchange, Max took a metal tray and smashed it against Rhea's face with brute force. She hit her again, and Rhea went down.

"You steal from me, bitch!" Max shouted.

Max continued her assault, slamming the metal tray against Rhea's face until it was covered with blood and her nose was broken. The clash provoked the other inmates with excitement. Screams broke out, and they cheered on the assault, but no one intervened.

The guards rushed forward, shouting orders, and disrupted the fight. However Max resisted, punching one guard in the face. She was taken down roughly and carried away.

Rhea was in bad shape. She was barely conscious, and her face was somewhat crooked. Because of the vicious assault on Rhea, numerous charges were brought up against Max. As she stood shackled in front of the warden while he berated her, something inside of her felt unconcerned. She liked who she was now—not one to be fucked with! If this were her a few years ago, then she wouldn't be in the position she was in now. If she'd stood up for herself— against Sandy, against Layla, even against Scottie— then things might have been different. But maybe this was her destiny.

Max had spent nearly five years in prison, and she'd adjusted and adapted. It was something she thought she would never do. Before Leanne's departure to a different prison, she'd taught Max everything she knew, and Max caught on quickly. She went from a meek sheep to a wolf, preying on the weak and humble.

After her ninety days in solitary confinement, Max stood naked in front of the guards feeling stronger than ever. They didn't break her. The guards handed her some clothing, told her to get dressed, and told her that the warden had some important news for her.

The news hit Max like a bolt of lightning. It damn near tore her apart emotionally. She couldn't believe it. Her father had passed away from a heart attack several weeks earlier. Max felt crushed. Because she had been in solitary, she didn't get the news immediately and couldn't even say goodbye. Her father meant the world to her, and now he was gone. Once again, her life was hell. She felt like that scared and panicky inmate from five years earlier. She didn't know what to do.

She wanted to contact her mother. *Oh God!* She thought about the nightmare her mother had to be going through, losing a daughter to a lengthy incarceration and a husband to a heart attack.

There was more news for Max, but Max couldn't take more bad news.

"You're being transferred. Your reputation and the environment of violence you've caused here has gotten out of hand. The paperwork was implemented during your time in confinement."

"Where am I going?" she asked dejectedly.

"Louisiana Correctional Institute for Women."

"Louisiana?"

Max was stunned she'd be so far from home. Now she'd never see her mother. Plus, she had to fight her way to the top in a new prison.

September 2014

Whistler parked his truck outside the 15-story building a block away from Central Park on 88th Street and hurried to the entrance. Lucky still wasn't answering her phone. He was worried. She needed to hear from him and not a stranger that her siblings were just murdered—gangland style—on their first day back to school.

He pushed in the code to enter the building and dashed through the lobby to the elevators and ascended to the top floor, where her three-bedroom, 986 sq. ft suite was located. Stepping out of the elevator, he removed his pistol.

He felt edgy. Everything felt so still. The hallway, bedecked with flowers, mirrors, and an antique table, was full of silence. He kept the gun ready by his side, and when he approached her door, he found it ajar. This worried him even more. Something was wrong.

Slowly, he pushed open the door and entered her residence. He found a turned-over table and some broken glass on the floor, and the place was empty.

"Shit!"

Whistler knew they'd already gotten to her. Once again, the killer or killers were one step ahead of them. How long had she been gone? Did her kidnappers leave anything behind? Was she still alive?

Whistler went looking around the apartment, and every room seemed disturbed. How did her captors know where to find her? How did they get inside the secure building? There were so many questions, but no answers.

His heart sank with apprehension and concern for Lucky. *Damn it!* If only he'd come earlier, he probably could have saved her. He probably would have killed them. He would have had a face and a name and, most likely, information about who was raging war against their organization.

Whistler knew he had to break the bad news to Scott. He took a deep breath and made the call to his boss. Scott's phone rang, and he answered.

"I'm at Lucky's place, and they took her, Scott—She's gone."

Wacka and Dagmar crossed over the Verrazano Bridge and entered Staten Island. The toll was paid, and they traveled on I-78 briefly and then exited onto a local road going south. Traffic was light during the warm night, a crescent moon in the sky. The two men were in a brown cargo van, driving at a moderate speed.

Wacka was smoking a Newport. Dagmar glanced into the back of the van, checking up on Lucky. She was on her side, bound at her wrists and ankles, and unconscious. They nabbed her in her short-shorts and bellybutton shirt.

"You hit that bitch too hard too many times, you think?" Dagmar asked. "Is she still breathing?"

"This bitch is crazy. She wouldn't cooperate—a fuckin' pit bull that bitch is."

Dagmar chuckled and pulled his attention away from Lucky. She wasn't going anywhere. "So what we gonna do with her?"

"What we were paid to do," Wacka said.

Wacka took a final pull from the cigarette and shared it with his friend. They continued to drive farther into Staten Island. They wanted to find a secluded place, where the abuse was to happen, and where they would be not interrupted. They knew who Lucky was, and they showed no worries about her father and his organization. They both were skilled ex-Marines.

Wacka did a short stint in the Marine Corps in his early twenties and made it to the rank of corporal. He soon was involved in an assault case against a twenty-three-year-old fellow Marine. The Marine accused Wacka—a.k.a. Marcus Garson—of brutally attacking him. Wacka was found guilty of first degree assault and stripped of his military rank and privileges. He was dishonorably discharged and received a ten-year sentence in Leavenworth.

Dagmar had received a bad conduct discharge from the military for serious offenses such as drug use, aggravated assault, and grand theft. He, too, did a sentence in Leavenworth, which was where he and Wacka connected.

They reached South Beach, a stretch of shoreline with a good amount of seclusion on the edge of Staten Island. Wacka killed the van's engine and turned his attention to Lucky.

She was just waking up. Her eyes struggled to open. She still felt the pain from where Wacka had repeatedly smashed the butt of the gun into the back of her head, creating a sizable gash. The brutal assault knocked her out cold.

Wacka smiled at his prize. "Wake up, bitch!"

He and Dagmar removed themselves from the front seat of the van and commenced a long-lasting assault.

Lucky found herself defenseless with her hands and ankles bound. She squirmed in her restraints as the two predators pounced on her with hard fists. "My father is gonna fuck y'all up!"

Her threats fell on deaf ears. Wacka punched her repeatedly in the face, spewing blood and bruising her skin. Meanwhile, Dagmar kicked her in the side.

Lucky cried and screamed. The blood saturated her face, blurring her vision. By now, she was disoriented, disheveled, bloody, and beaten. Her right eye had been hit so many times, it was swollen shut, and her eye socket and ribs were broken. They beat her within an inch of her life.

When they were done with her, they removed her battered body from the van and dumped her on the beach, barely breathing.

"Why we're keeping her alive?" Dagmar asked. "Why she's different from the others?"

"Because our employer wants us to send a message with this one," Wacka said.

Dagmar didn't like that she'd seen their faces. He gripped a 9mm in his hand and glared at Lucky slumped against the sand under the cover of night. He pointed the gun at her. "She needs to go!"

"We chill, Dagmar. You hear me? Stand the fuck down!" Wacka said to him. "This bitch don't know anything about us."

Dagmar griped, but it was Wacka's show, so he relented.

They went back to the van, leaving Lucky on the beach in need of serious medical treatment. Once again, she was unconscious with life-threatening injuries.

"I got a bad feeling about this one," Dagmar continued. "We need to break out."

"Let's blow this town then. I'll go to DC and see Moms," Wacka said.

It would be hours before Lucky was found by a man walking his dog. At just eighteen years old, she probably would never be the same.

Upon hearing the news, Scott and Whistler hurried to Staten Island University Hospital South Campus on Sequine Avenue. They came in full force; almost a small and heavily armed army flanked them. Hearing the grim news about his daughter's nasty assault plunged Scott into a darker and unstable state. He couldn't believe it'd happened again. They had gotten to Lucky somehow and done things to her he didn't want to think about.

Scott and Whistler marched through the hospital lobby with a sense of urgency. They knew her room number, and security didn't dare get in their way. Scott looked like the Devil himself, scarlet with rage, wearing a mean scowl. His fists were clenched, and he wanted to start World War III on the streets of New York and beyond. Nobody was safe.

Lucky was in the ICU, her face swollen up like a pumpkin and almost unrecognizable. She suffered several facial fractures—broken cheekbone, jaw, nose, and eye socket. She was connected to tubes and wires, a monitor, and ventilator.

Scott stood over his beaten daughter transfixed with more heartache. Unable to compose himself, a few tears trickled from his eyes. Seeing Lucky beaten like that tore him apart. Whistler too. Both men were in bad shape. The emotions engulfed them with intense feelings of failure and culpability.

Scott squeezed his fists tighter, feeling his skin break from the pressure against his fingernails. "I want them all dead, Whistler. Every last muthafucka in DMC's crew, wiped out immediately," Scott said.

"These attacks—they feel personal, Scott. I'm not so sure it was DMC," Whistler said.

Scott suddenly spun around and charged at Whistler, grabbed him up by his clothing, and forced him against the wall. "Where the fuck was you? Huh? You tell me this is personal! It's fuckin' personal all right; they're coming after my family! I want every soldier—every associate—on the hunt for these bastards! I want 'em dead! I want their families and their children dead too! I want them fuckin' exterminated!" Scott released his tight grip from his friend. "Get it done!"

Whistler collected himself, understanding Scott's emotions. He fixed his ruffled clothing and heaved a sigh.

Scott was back at his daughter's bedside, standing in silence and woe.

Two suit-and-tie detectives showed up at the hospital to get a statement from Lucky, but she was in no condition to talk. Scott and Whistler were like two snarling guard dogs toward the detectives. Scott made it clear that no one would be speaking to his little girl. He didn't care if they wore a badge or not. Besides, no one in his organization spoke to police.

Scott sent the detectives on their way, away from his daughter's room. "You talk to my lawyers, not my peoples."

Layla showed up at the hospital in worse shape than her husband. She was devastated with anguish and felt like it was ripping her apart. When she saw Lucky, she shrieked in agony and nearly collapsed. She couldn't take any more. Why were they targeting her kids? What was her husband doing about it? Losing Gotti was painful enough, but losing more of her children was an apocalypse.

Bugsy and Meyer arrived from Wilmington hours after Layla, and they were furious. Bugsy's blasé and unruffled demeanor had become ruffled, and he was ready to blow someone's head off. Meyer's violent behavior was amplified tenfold. He was a bomb ready to explode and take out an entire city block. He wanted bloodshed. He wanted muthafuckas' heads impaled with sharp spears for everyone to see. Niggas touched Bonnie, Clyde, and Lucky all on the same day? Unbelievable.

The doctor came into the room with grim news. Lucky had suffered severe blunt force trauma to the head, and there was some swelling in her brain. She was in a medically induced coma, receiving a controlled dose of anesthetic. She was touch-and-go and would be observed vigilantly for the next twenty-four to forty-eight hours. The doctor told them if there were no signs of improvement, she might be brain-dead.

The news was a crushing blow to the family.

"You're saying our sister might be brain-dead?" Bugsy asked.

"It's too early to tell. The swelling prevents blood, and oxygen, from reaching the brain. The anesthetic should do its job, but there's nothing I can do until the swelling has reduced. At that point we will run some tests on her and determine if surgery is necessary."

"What kind of tests?" Scott asked.

"We'll employ a nuclear brain scan or a cerebral angiogram, where a radioactive tracer is injected into the vein to see if blood is going to the brain," the doctor said.

The word *radioactive* stirred up some alarm to everyone in the room.

"What do you mean radioactive?" Bugsy asked.

"It's a safe procedure," the doctor assured them.

"It better be," Scott chimed.

"And what's the second test?" Bugsy asked him.

"The cerebral angiogram is when the dye is injected into an artery, and X-ray pictures are taken of the brain. Now typically, four major arteries supply a lot of blood to the brain. In a brain-dead person, the X-ray of the blood vessels shows no blood going to the brain at all."

Meyer got in the doctor's face with a threatening stare. "You do whatever you need to fix her, Doc. That's my fuckin' sister."

Hearing the possibility of her daughter being brain-dead, Layla flew out the room in tears. She couldn't hear any more news.

Scott stood firm but saddened. Though Lucky was in bad shape, he didn't take his eyes off her. He took her still hand in his and vowed there would be vengeance executed in her honor.

Whistler loitered outside the lobby smoking a cigarette. It was hard to see Lucky in that horrid condition. She was far from the sexy diva he was used to. Her beautiful face was a complete mess.

Scott instructed Whistler to scrap their plans of a shrewd takeover in Delaware in exchange for extreme bloodshed and warfare. Something in Whistler screamed that they were barking up the wrong tree. They were missing something. He knew it.

I t was a beautiful September Saturday, with a broad blue sky and a bright sun. Detective Jones was up bright and early and neatly dressed for work. He holstered his weapon on his hip and secured his police badge before brewing a cup of coffee and watching the morning news in the kitchen. His interest was mostly in the stock market, as he'd recently acquired some stock and wanted to invest his money wisely to launder his illegal income.

On the streets, business was still good. The money was pouring in greater than before with the new management, and things were operating smoothly. As requested, the new organization was keeping the bloodshed to a minimum.

His dealings with Deuce were gradually fading, as he didn't want to end his business with DMC abruptly and bring on suspicion of his betrayal. But the inevitable was to come for Deuce. Nice and slow, Detective Jones allowed the new organization to move into Delaware territory with minimum collateral damage. And their product was far superior to DMC's.

He sat at the kitchen table drinking his coffee and observing the Dow Jones. His stock was up by 5%. So far, life was good.

His beautiful wife entered the kitchen dressed in a purple nightgown, and they kissed each other good morning. The kids were still sleeping. It gave the couple a moment of intimacy before the start of his workday and an awakened family.

Jones cupped his wife's ample ass, and their lips locked. "You trying to have me take the day off?"

She winked. "It depends on how loaded your gun is."

He chuckled. "Sharp rounds . . . accurate, able to penetrate anything."

"I think I might need some quick penetrating then," she replied.

"You do, huh?"

"Uh-huh." She was wrapped in his strong arms, feeling his erection growing. She loved him, and he may have been a corrupt, dirty, murderous cop, but he was a loving husband and father.

She pulled herself away from her husband's loving grasp and continued to smile at him. "Come upstairs into the bedroom, and I'll give you a real good-morning kiss." She disappeared from his view and exited the kitchen.

Jones figured he had enough time for a quickie. He made his way to the bedroom, already unbuckling his pants.

The door was ajar. However, walking into the bedroom, he received the shock of his life. Luna had his wife in his arms with a Glock 17 to her temple. If she moved wrong, her brains would paint the bedroom.

Detective Jones reached for his holstered weapon, but he was abruptly taken down by several armed goons, including Meyer. His face was forcibly pushed against the floor. His gun was removed from the holster and the barrel thrust to the back of his head.

"Chill, muthafucka! We here to talk—unless you make it something else," Meyer warned him. "I got goons in each of your children's rooms, and unless you want them to wake up with a bang, I suggest you fully cooperate."

"Fuck you!" Jones growled.

"Really? Fuck us when we got a gun to your wife's head and one to yours too? You sure you wanna play this tough-guy role?"

Jones squirmed against the men holding him down, but he wasn't

196

strong enough to free himself. How did they get into his house? How did they know where he lived?

"I thought we had a deal," Jones cried out.

"We still do. I just want you to tell us where to find Deuce and his family," Meyer said.

"I don't know anything!"

"You're a cop—you know everything. You think we're stupid?" Meyer glanced at Luna, giving him a thin signal.

Luna cocked back the hammer to the pistol against the wife's head. They weren't bluffing.

"No! No!" Jones screamed.

"Talk, or we'll start decorating this place with your family's blood," Meyer said.

"Okay," Jones uttered. "He has a younger sister in Baltimore; it's his only family."

"See, now we're getting somewhere," Meyer mocked.

It took less than ten minutes of interrogation for Detective Jones to tell them everything he knew about Deuce's peoples, mostly about the few living family members he had. He knew little, but it was enough information for Meyer and Luna to act on.

Jones fumed that Meyer and his goons had the audacity to break into his home, endanger his children, and hold his wife hostage. They'd gone too far. It took him hours to calm down his wife.

Mica's breathing was ragged. She couldn't take any more. Her body ached and her eyes watered with pain and fear, but there was much more to come. Her apartment was torn apart by the sudden intruders. Too many niggas to count surrounded her and tortured her like it was their right.

Mica was a lovely young woman, or used to be—until they went to work on her. She resided in luxury in a three-bedroom condo by the Baltimore harbor. There were perks to being Deuce's little sister.

But now came the disadvantages. Her face beaten and her body bruised, the goons were drooling like hound dogs, excited for revenge.

"Please . . . I don't know anything," she pleaded with her attackers. She was cemented to the floor on all fours, her dark flesh barely covered and her tears plentiful.

"Bitch, we don't expect you to know anything," Luna said. "We're just gettin' started." He walked toward her with a sharp knife in his hand.

This was his expertise—pain and more pain. He grabbed her by her long dreads and dragged her across the floor like a rag doll. When she kicked and screamed, he punched her in the face with his black latex gloves, and blood gushed from her nose.

Then his goons held her down and left her face exposed.

Luna took the knife to her skin, becoming a barbaric surgeon. It was extreme, excruciating pain. He literally ripped her face apart. Flaps of skin hung from her cheeks and forehead. There was lots of blood, and Mica squirmed violently in her captors' grip, but the torture continued until there were pieces of her face scattered everywhere. Luna had cut parts of her almost down to the bone. The grisly scene even made a few of his men squeamish.

When Luna was done with her, she was barely alive and looked horrendous. There was nothing lovely about her anymore. Her torture was to be a message to Deuce. But there were more horrible things to come.

Luna stood over the suffering girl and smiled. The way she looked, she might as well be dead.

"We need to finish this up, Luna. Meyer wants everyone dead," one of the men said.

Luna nodded. Since he'd started with a knife, he would end her life with the same knife that had grossly disfigured her. He crouched toward the victim, took her head into his hand, looked her in the eyes deeply, and gradually plunged the knife into her throat, like it was sinking into quicksand.

There was a sudden jerking movement from Mica, as the sharp blade pierced through her neck and drained her life. Luna felt her soul depart as her body slowly went limp in his arms.

They left the macabre scene for somebody to find.

Their hunt for DMC was to continue. Mica was only the beginning.

Moe, one of DMC's ranking soldiers, sat in the barbershop chair in West Baltimore laughing it up with the barbers and clientele, discussing big-booty video girls. The flat-screen television perched in the corner of the shop showed the latest Miami rap video with beautiful, bikini-dressed girls twerking on the beach and lounging on exotic cars.

Moe stated, "I been there and done that."

"Yeah, right, nigga. You been where? To the local strip clubs and done them cheap hoes wit' bullet and stab wounds?" a customer named Bird countered.

The barbershop roared with laughter.

Moe threw up his middle finger. "You wish you were me, nigga."

"No, nigga, your girl wishes you were me."

"Yo, Bird, fuck you! You wide-nose, yellow-teeth, gumbo-lookin' muthafucka!"

There was more laughter from the men inside the barbershop.

"Damn, Moe, your feelings are hurt? I'm just sayin', your girl about to take you out the game and bench your ass for missing them dunks. But I'm Jordan on the courts. I stay layin' it in."

Moe reached into his pocket and pulled out a wad of cash, mostly hundreds and fifties. "Nigga, when you get money like me, you can have any bitch you want. Matter of fact, I'll pay for your haircut too, nigga! Yo, your hair looks like it's really hurtin' right now, screaming, 'Help me, help me!' You over there lookin' like *The Jungle Book*."

Moe tossed a hundred-dollar bill on the floor. "Oh, and tell your moms I can't pay her rent anymore, so you might be evicted too."

The two men wisecracked on each other back and forth. It was routine. There wasn't a day at the barbershop without jokes, talking sports, womanizing, and having some good old-fashioned fun.

It was a regular Saturday morning. The barbershop was busy with patrons waiting on the four barbers. They entertained themselves by watching TV, messing their phones, reading, or indulging in the shop talk.

Moe felt at home at the barbershop. Everyone there knew he was a gun nigga with DMC and very dangerous, but at the barbershop, he was sociable. He joked around with the barbers and the other patrons. And he was a generous tipper.

Moe sat comfortable in the chair while his barber shaped up the back of his head. He was armed but felt secure. West Baltimore was his stomping grounds. It had been his home, and he had been getting his weekly haircut at Nappy Cuts on N. Howard Street for years. A father of three kids with two baby mamas, Moe took pride in his appearance, from his clothing to his vehicle. His black Mercedes S-Class was parked outside the barbershop.

"How's life?" his barber asked.

"Crazy, Flip. We got soldiers goin' MIA. Niggas don't know where the fuck they went. Three of our peoples just gone, just like that. We don't know if they dead, locked up, or what," Moe said. "Deuce is goin' crazy over this shit."

"Just be careful out there."

"Twenty-four seven, my nigga, I stay wit' mine," Moe said, referring to his gun.

Flip was finishing Moe up. They laughed and talked. Everything was normal until it wasn't normal.

Two masked men burst into the shop, pistols drawn. The barbershop quickly spun into a panic, as patrons frantically hit the floor and chaos ensued.

Moe desperately tried to reach for his 9mm tucked into his waistband, but he was too late.

The gunmen aimed their .45s at Moe and opened fire. *Bam! Bam! Bam! Bam! Bam!*

Several bullets pierced his chest and stomach, and Moe promptly slumped dead in the barber chair.

Just as quickly as they had come, the gunmen left, leaving behind a dead DMC soldier.

Luna and Meyer drove north on the New Jersey Turnpike. It was an hour after midnight, and the traffic was flowing freely on a calm, full-moon night. Meyer was in a foul mood because earlier they had just laid Bonnie and Clyde to rest in the same mausoleum as Gotti. Once again it was a grand affair. Both children had lacquer white caskets trimmed in 24 karat gold. Doves were released, harps played, and everyone sobbed. Lucky was still in the hospital fucked up and might be there through October.

Luna was smoking a Newport and listening to Meyer curse out one female caller after the next until he found one that piqued his interest.

He soon ended the call with a smile. "I really like this one."

Luna remained nonchalant. "You like 'em all."

"Nah, this one is different."

"Different until you fuck 'em."

Meyer laughed. "Shit, pussy keeps the sanity flowing. I gotta keep busy, my nigga. I got a lot on my mind. Lucky's taking Bonnie and Clyde personally, and Pops is still dissin' me."

"Well, hopefully, tonight will help with that."

"I think it will."

Luna nodded as he navigated the Lexus off the Turnpike and traveled to Pine Barrens, a wooded area stretching across southern New Jersey. In Pine Barrens, people and things could easily get lost.

It was a long drive to the secluded location. They traveled into darker, more isolated territory with narrow, rocky trails and more woods. Satisfied with the surroundings, Luna stopped the car and killed the ignition.

Both men climbed out the Lexus, and Luna opened the trunk. He shined a light on the incapacitated Jo-Jo, who was tied up. He was one of Deuce's feared enforcers, but now he was in their grasp.

"Look at you, nigga. What y'all did to my brothers and sisters, I could kill you twice," Meyer growled.

"Fuck you!" Jo-Jo shouted back.

Meyer smashed the butt of his gun into his face, churning out more blood.

Jo-Jo was immobile with a black-and-blue face. He frowned at his attackers. As a man who'd killed so many people for Deuce, he knew fate had caught up to him. He lived by the gun, and now he would die by the gun. "We never touched your fuckin' family, nigga. Ya brothers could eat a dick, and ya sisters could suck one, nigga," he said.

"You lie to live, nigga." Meyer pointed the Smith & Wesson 457 at Jo-Jo's head, and with images of his murdered siblings and beaten sister, he released his rage into their captive.

Boom! Boom! Boom! Boom! Boom!

All five shots were fired into Jo-Jo's face. His blood pooled inside the trunk, which was lined with a thick plastic tarp, making it easier to remove the body and not leave behind any blood evidence.

Meyer had fucked him up. It was a sight to see—a man with his face shot to shit, his brains and flesh exposed. They were immune to the horrible sight. Murder was a commonplace thing for them. It wasn't a job, it was a necessity.

They removed the body from the trunk, wrapped it in the tarp, and carried it deep into the woods. They came across a small ravine and tossed Jo-Jo's body into it. It was miles and miles away from any public road and any civilization. They left him there for the animals to feast on.

Before walking away, Meyer spat at the dead body and frowned. "Bitch-ass nigga!"

"We need to go," Luna said.

They turned and traveled back as they came, their flashlights dancing in the dark, guiding them through the thick and wide woods where one false move could lead them astray. They made it back to the Lexus, their mission completed.

Jo-Jo was one of the several goons from DMC they'd made disappear. They were burying bodies from Delaware to Baltimore, where they would never be found.

The Pine Barrens trip was their second trip. A day earlier, they had discarded two of DMC's men in the wooded area. Others, like Moe, were executed in public to make a statement.

31

Rock's head hung low and wobbly. His body was secured to the chair with several long chains wrapped around his torso. His arms were tied behind him, and his legs felt numb and rubbery. His mouth was full of blood, and his eyes were so swollen, he could hardly see from them. Everything was blurry. The pain was unbearable.

A giant fist smashed into the side of his face, and more than a few teeth flew out of his mouth. He was hit again, and again, and again until the man striking him felt satisfied.

"You betray me, muthafucka!" the attacker shouted. "Tell me something, Rock."

"I don't know nothin'. Please . . . I'm a victim too, Deuce." Rock felt the urge to collapse to the ground, but his restraints were keeping him up.

Deuce struck him again. The blow damn near took Rock's head off. His head thrashed around violently, and he whimpered from the pain.

"You think I'm a fool, Rock? What's going on in Delaware? My money's low—real fuckin' low—and I got soldiers disappearing. Who's making a move on me?"

"Deuce, I promise . . . I don't know. I'm just as in the dark as you."

"Really, Rock? But word on the streets is you're moving new product, nice quality for an excellent price. How's that?"

Rock was stuck on stupid. The organization with superior product to move wasn't there to protect him from Deuce.

"I don't know names, Deuce . . . these people . . . they're smart," Rock said.

"Smart, huh? You dick-riding? Huh? Who are they? I want a name."

There was no name for Rock to give. He worked with one person, who he only knew as X. He was Rock's supplier. They met twice a month to re-up. There was no conversation and no information to give, besides to let Deuce know that their product sold faster than pancakes at IHOP.

"They came into my home and threatened me, Deuce. I swear to you, this ain't me!"

Deuce struck him again with mighty blow that could have broken his neck. Instead, it mutilated his face more and almost made his eyes protrude from his skull. His blood drizzled onto the floor, his body ravaged with destruction.

"Tell me something, muthafucka!" Deuce yelled.

In the room with Deuce watching the coercive interrogation was Jimmy, Deuce's right-hand man. He stood six two with an athletic physique and looked intimidating with chiseled features and cold eyes. He stood silently behind Deuce, dressed in a black-and-white Nike tracksuit and wearing an intense scowl aimed at Rock. He wanted a piece of Rock too, but it was Deuce's show. Jimmy had ways of making people talk.

"You're toying with him, Deuce," Jimmy said.

Deuce spun around, frowning. "I got this, nigga. When I need you to bite, then I'll take off your leash."

Jimmy simply shrugged, not offended by the statement.

Deuce turned his attention back to Rock. "I can do this all night with you, Rock."

Deuce's tattooed arms were massive, the space between his biceps and his triceps looked a mile apart, and he had a broad chest. He used to be a boxer and had once competed in the Golden Gloves. At a bulky six three, he could easily be mistaken for the Hulk if he was green.

Ten minutes later, Rock had a broken jaw and a fractured skull from the repeated punches to his face. There was no more use for Rock. It was time to end the pain. The man had no useful information to give to them.

Deuce situated himself behind Rock's seated and severely beaten frame and wrapped his powerful arms around Rock's neck in an aggressive chokehold. He applied pressure and squeezed tight, making Rock feel like a python had wrapped around him. He crushed Rock's windpipe and snapped his neck with no trouble. Rock lay slumped in the chair. He was dead, and Deuce had barely broken a sweat.

Deuce looked at Jimmy. "Muthafuckas are trying to shut us down, Jimmy."

"We need to shut them down," Jimmy said.

"First we need to know who the fuck they are."

"I can find out."

"You need to do that . . . find out who's killing off my crew and turning my peoples against me. I'm losing money, time, and soldiers. I want to return the favor to these muthafuckas tenfold."

Jimmy nodded and crossed his arms. "Consider it done."

ayla drank in silence and misery. She'd cried so long and so hard, she felt like she had no more tears in her eyes. The bedroom was dark, the house was empty, and things felt unnatural. With Lucky still in the hospital fighting for her life, three of her children dead, and someone declaring war on her family, her life had quickly gone from fortunate to disastrous. She couldn't look for support and comfort from her husband, since their marriage was rocky and their relationship seemed to be deteriorating. Scott had disappeared mostly, supposedly on the hunt for the animals that murdered and assaulted their kids, and grieving by himself somewhere.

Layla finished her bottle of E&J. The dark liquor reminded her of her younger days and made her feel violent and sadistic. She didn't want to be alone, but she accepted it. And she didn't want to look and feel helpless. She was from Brooklyn. Her life had never been easy, and she would not sit around and cry every day. She'd done enough of that. She had grieved for her children long enough.

Layla felt she needed to get back on her gangster shit. She'd tried to go legit. She wanted to build her own business, start a new life, and play nice with the white people, but the unforgiving streets had caught up to her. So she decided to be unforgiving herself. Everybody was a suspect in her eyes, and everybody had a role in killing her children.

When Maxine had called collect to give her condolences, Layla wasn't in the mood to receive sympathy from anyone. Happy-go-lucky Layla was no longer feeling so generous toward Maxine and her problems. Layla no longer wanted to send the cash to protect her friend. She had her own problems to deal with. There were some loose ends she needed to tie up.

Scott would handle things his way, and she'd handle things her way.

She met with her two sons, Meyer and Bugsy. In the reunion, she gave them an address. "I want everyone at this location taken care of ASAP. Leave no one alive. I want to send a message."

Meyer nodded, amped to execute more people. He was itching to implement bloodshed and get payback for Lucky, Bonnie, Clyde, and Gotti by any means necessary. Whoever needed to go would go. He didn't ask questions. He and Luna were on a successful hunt in Delaware and Baltimore, where five of Deuce's men were killed and never heard from again.

Meyer held a Washington, DC address in his hand, where Layla had been sending the money for Maxine's protection. Layla wanted her reach to stretch far inside the Louisiana jail to protect her longtime friend. Now the shit was about to hit the fan and fly everywhere.

Meyer, Luna, and two other gunmen sat outside the Frederick Douglass Garden Apartments in Southeast DC on a chilly night in October. The cold weather was approaching, but frozen hearts were already present. Meyer and Luna felt right at home in the violent, crime-ridden area. They plotted inside the Dodge Durango and smoked cigarettes and observed. They watched everything around them—the residents and their movements. There was no telling who was who. Anyone could be a threat, so they weren't taking any chances. All four men came heavily armed—Luna with a double-barrel sawed-off shotgun and a pistol in his waistband. Meyer came prepared with two Smith & Wesson SW99s, and Nifco and X-Ray were armed with Glock 19s.

They exited the Durango and walked toward the three-story building where Shiniquia's mother lived. They split up, Luna and Meyer going one way and Nifco and X-Ray a different way. They did their best to look inconspicuous. The late hour made it easier, since there were no kids playing, no old folks loitering outside, and not many witnesses in the area. The local thugs were a block away gambling, and the local dealers were busy with customers.

The men were in black, and upon entering the lobby, they masked up. They had little information to go on, only knowing the building and apartment number of Shiniquia's mother. She had two kids, a boy and a girl. The son was nicknamed Wacka. Meyer had never heard of him, but word on the streets was he was a head case and a terrifying bad-ass.

Meyer and Luna waited near the stairwell with their guns out. This had to be quick and accurate. They'd rush into the apartment, kill everyone inside, and get out of the building alive. Knowing they were in foreign territory, their heads repeatedly swiveled, keeping an eye out for threats.

A short moment later, Nifco and X-Ray met up with them holding the superintendent at gunpoint. Nifco and X-Ray had kicked open his basement door and snatched him out of bed wearing just his underwear. The middle-aged man was sniveling, ready to piss himself, and he was willing to do whatever they asked of him.

They led the super to the target's apartment on the third floor. He had the keys, so they used him to access the apartment without detection. All four men stood poised by the door, and Meyer had his gun to the superintendent's head as he opened the apartment door.

They heard music playing from the apartment as the door opened slowly, and all four men crept into the apartment like ninjas in the night.

Meyer took the lead with a gun in each hand. He moved toward the kitchen, where he heard the most activity and the music. Luna followed, poised with the shotgun.

Without hesitating, Meyer emerged out the blue, arms outstretched with guns, shocking a man and older female counting money at the table. They were wide-eyed with terror.

Meyer opened fire first. *Bak! Bak!* He struck the male at the table, and he went down quickly.

The female tried to flee into the adjacent hallway, but Luna quickly cut her down in the back with the shotgun. *Chk-chk! Boom!* The blast tore through the woman's back, ripped through her abdomen, and sent her flying across the kitchen, her body mangled from the massive blast.

"Muthafuckas!" the men heard from one bedroom, and suddenly there was gunfire. *Bam! Bam! Bam! Bam!*

The shots splintered the door near Meyer, missing his head by inches. He was lucky to be alive. He quickly pivoted and returned fire.

A shootout ensued, and two unknown men that emerged from the bedroom weren't backing down.

Bak! Bak! Bak!

Pop! Pop!

X-Ray went down with a bullet to his head.

Luna cut loose with the shotgun and sprayed the hallway, creating large craters inside the walls, but they were pinned down near the kitchen. Whoever it was, they were well armed and giving them one hell of a fight. Meyer and Luna weren't expecting retaliation.

"Fuck you, niggas! Fuck you, muthafuckas!" Wacka shouted madly. His .50-cal. became a beast in his hand. His moms had been shot down like a dog in the kitchen. And so was his cousin. Now it was he and Dagmar under siege. But then that quickly changed when Dagmar caught two in the chest and went down.

Wacka took coverage in the bedroom, bullets zipping by him. He wasn't going out like that. He did not understand the masked intruders, but he was ready to kill every last one.

"Y'all muthafuckas killed my moms! Y'all killed my moms!" Wacka chanted. He flung himself from his crouching area by the doorframe and fired madly at the encroaching threats. *Bak! Bak! Bak! Bak! Bak!*

But then he felt a sharp sting on his side. He had been hit. He caught another bullet to his stomach and stumbled. *Shit!* He was out of options, and there wasn't anywhere to go.

But then he saw his opportunity. Wounded and under heavy gunfire, Wacka took off running and smashed through the bedroom window, doing a Superman from the third floor.

Meyer and the others went to the window. They couldn't believe it. Shot twice, the nigga jumped from the third floor, and he was still mobile and shooting back at them.

Wacka had landed roughly on the ground, and he was hurt badly. Seeing Meyer peeking his head from out the window, Wacka lifted the gun and shot at him. *Bak! Bak!* He missed, but it gave him a window to escape. He stumbled away and disappeared around the corner.

"Shit! Meyer shouted.

"We need to go!" Luna shouted.

The shootout left four dead, including X-Ray. They fled from the crime scene, descending the stairwell and erupting from the building in haste. Police sirens blared in the distance. Though they'd missed one, three out of four wasn't bad. And Wacka could run, but he couldn't hide.

Meyer was only following orders from his mother. Why she wanted these people dead, he didn't ask. He was already filled with rage and hatred, so killing anyone let him blow off some steam.

33

"What? No! No!" Shiniquia cried out in shock as she clutched the phone receiver tighter. When she couldn't get in contact with her mother, she called her uncle, Kenny. She couldn't believe the news that her family had been executed. Her mother and her cousin were dead.

"Wacka was there, Shiniquia. He got hit up too."

"Is he all right?"

"I don't know. He took two slugs and said he couldn't go to the hospital afraid he'd get locked up. He sounded fucked up, in pain, and his breathing was shallow."

Shiniquia was distraught. She couldn't lose her brother too. She screamed, "Where is he, Kenny!"

"I think that nigga dead."

"Did he say who did this?"

"Nah, he didn't. He just said niggas came through poppin' off shots."

The home invasion and homicides at the Frederick Douglass Garden Apartments had made the evening news and the front page of several DC newspapers. The paper listed the government names of two individuals: Donovan Magner, who Shiniquia knew as Dagmar, and Xavier Bernard, whom she didn't know. She didn't know if Xavier was friend or foe.

Shiniquia was overwhelmed with grief but did her best to keep it together. She thought it had to be Layla. She hurried to see Max to give her the horrifying news. They met in the dayroom, where Max was seated, watching TV and having a private talk with one of her minions.

Shiniquia rushed over. "We need to talk!"

Max looked up at her friend and saw the sense of urgency and pain on her face. She got up and walked away with Shiniquia to talk privately.

"My family's dead," Shiniquia said. Once again, tears flooded her eyes.

Max was taken aback by the news. "What?"

"They're all dead, Max. My mother, cousin, and I think Wacka too!"

"Dead? How?"

"It was a home invasion. Their murders made the local papers. You think Layla and Scott had anything to do wit' this? Did they find out about my brother?"

"No. I don't think so."

If Layla had found out about them, then why were she and Shiniquia still alive? No, there had to be another reason Shiniquia's family was killed. She was certain that Layla knew nothing about the conspiracy Maxine had enacted. They'd been extra careful, and if Wacka was the proficient killer that Shiniquia proclaimed he was, then there was no way he would have fucked up.

"The news said someone named Xavier was involved. He was murdered on the scene, and I don't know if he was wit' my brother or against him. Xavier could be the enemy. When you speak with Layla see if she knows him."

"Look, I know you in your bag of feelings right now, but if I mention that nigga's name then I'm sending a message loud and clear to Layla that I set up those hits. And if she has any doubts on whether I'm involved then my meddling into what happened to your peoples would get me killed."

"I can't let this go, Max."

"You need to chill."

"What if this bitch is plotting on us too?

"Your brother got enemies, don't he?" Max said.

"Yeah, but—"

"Shiniquia, my condolences to your family, but I don't believe this was Layla. Only two people in this prison know the arrangement we have, you and me, and out there, Wacka. I've kept my mouth shut, and I know you're not talking. And your brother is a loose cannon, from my understanding. So I believe they came for him for other reasons."

Shiniquia felt Max could be right, but her family was still dead. She sobbed. She wanted to go home. She wanted to see her mother. She wanted to attend the funeral. In two years she was going up for parole on her lengthy sentence, and she was eager to reconnect with her family.

"That was my moms. Why they do her like that?" she cried out.

Max did her best to console her friend. But what was a bigger tragedy to her was that her hit man Wacka could be dead. Max found her plan dead in the water, stranded out at sea with no lifeboat and no sail. She needed a plan B, and she needed it fast. She had come too far to have everything come to a screeching halt.

"Maxine, on the line in fifteen. You got a visitor," the correction officer shouted.

Max was taken aback by the news. It was a week after they'd received the tragic news about Shiniquia's family, and she was trying to figure shit out. Louisiana was too far away from New York for anyone to make the trip. Max could only think of one person with the means and the time to come visit her in Louisiana. It had to be Layla. But she had never come to visit, so why now?

It sent a panic through Max. Something was up. Layla was in Louisiana for a reason, and it probably wasn't good.

Max had to quickly change her appearance. She needed to soften her hard image. Layla couldn't see her this way. She had to see the Maxine she'd known from twenty years earlier.

With Shiniquia's and another inmate's help, they hurriedly took out Maxine's cornrows and combed out her hair into a bushy Afro and then into a thick ponytail. She needed to look soft and feminine.

Time was running out.

Max stood up, looked at Shiniquia, and said, "Hit me."

"What?" Shiniquia was shocked. "What you mean hit you?"

"I want you to punch me in the eye really hard."

"Max, are you crazy?"

"Shiniquia, just do it!"

Shiniquia tightened her fist and thrust it forward at Max's right eye. It hurt, but it didn't do much damage.

"Do it again," Max said.

Shiniquia looked reluctant, but she knew Max had a reason for the attack. The second punch hurt more than the first, but it did the trick. Max had a slight black eye. It was believable.

The second inmate was confused, but she kept her comment and questions to herself.

Max applied some lipstick to her lips and puckered them in the mirror. She looked almost like her old self, and with the black eye, she looked more sheep than the wolf she'd become after doing twenty years inside.

Max entered the full visiting room and looked around for Layla. She soon spotted her long-lost frenemy seated across the room. She was alone and looking like a hustler's wife, her long sensuous hair falling down past her shoulders. Though they talked via phone and wrote letters, it'd been nearly twenty years since they'd physically seen each other.

She and Layla finally locked eyes, creating an awkward moment between them. Max approached, and Layla stood up from the table. For a moment, there was silence—not a hug and not an apology—and stares of awkwardness as each lady took in the other's physical appearance. Layla looked the same, just prettier and wealthier, while Maxine was dressed in her prison officials and needed a drastic makeover.

They took a seat opposite of each other. Max glanced at the room and saw the female inmates with their children and their loved ones. It was her first visit, and things felt odd. She saw the smiles on the girls' faces. Having a piece of home coming to see them regularly was therapeutic.

Layla zeroed in on Maxine's swollen eye. *This girl will never stand up for herself,* Layla thought, feeling sorry for her friend.

"It's been a long time, Layla."

"It has."

"My condolences on your loss," Max said, sounding sincere. "When I heard, it messed me up."

"Well, my children's murders won't go unpunished."

Max wanted to know what she meant by the statement, but she couldn't fish for information. She had to play it cool and appear timid.

"What brings you to Louisiana, Layla?" Max asked.

Before Layla could answer her, a rough, butch looking inmate looked at Max and said, "Max, I know I'm late, but I got that for you tomorrow. We cool, right?"

Max only looked at her. She didn't respond.

The exchange baffled Layla, but she shook it off.

"I know it's been a long time, Maxine. You've been on my mind lately," Layla said. "What happened to your eye?"

"A fight."

"Did you win?" Layla joked.

"I'm not a fighter, Layla. You know that."

"Twenty years inside, Maxine, an' you still letting people punk you. When will you get tired of it an' do something about it?"

Max sighed. "I'm just tired."

"Well, I came to tell you personally—" Layla started.

"Tell me what personally?"

"The problem that you're having inside here, it's being handled as we speak, from out there to in here. I'm sorry I didn't take care of it sooner for you."

It didn't take long for Max to understand what she meant. *Shiniquia!* Layla had her family murdered, and Shiniquia was probably next.

Max said nothing and kept her facial expression neutral, but inside she was panicking. She had the urge to bolt from the visiting area and warn Shiniquia, but she couldn't move. She could show no signs of guilt or remorse and had to remain deadpan while looking at Layla.

"You can say thank you," Layla said smugly.

Max wanted to rip her fuckin' throat out.

Shiniquia walked from the dayroom to the cafeteria in a single file with several other inmates, one guard leading them. She felt the attack from behind out the blue—many arms yanking her into a nearby room and closing the door. The other inmates kept things moving, knowing to mind their business.

In the small room, Shiniquia was surrounded by three scowling inmates, each gripping a shank. She didn't understand what was happening. Why were they after her?

"Y'all bitches suicidal, stupid, or crazy? Which one?" Shiniquia shouted.

They had no time for words. They were there to do a job and do it swiftly.

Shiniquia soon felt the sharp tip of the shank plunged into the side of her neck, and blood gushed from the staggering jab. She then felt a second shank thrust into her chest, followed by the third sinking into her neck again. The stabbing was repetitive and violent until she collapsed on the floor, choking on her own blood, which pooled underneath her. She was dead.

The inmates discarded their weapons and retreated from the scene.

Max finally made it back from the visiting room and learned that Shiniquia had been stabbed to death near the dayroom. No witnesses. Layla had that far of a reach.

Max was beside herself with grief. Pangs of hatred resurfaced, and she needed to regroup. Her best friend had been viciously murdered, and Layla had sanctioned the hit. Money bought everything. Layla's visit somehow was a ploy, maybe meant to be a distraction. Max didn't know what or how much Layla knew. She knew she had to watch her back. She was still feared and respected, but who would dare kill her best friend?

2015

Layla stood in the center of her masterpiece, and she felt some content. The Florida compound was finally finished, and everything looked spectacular, just the way she predicted. It was a costly project, in the tens of millions, but well worth the cost and the time. There would be three homes set up as shrines to remember Gotti, Bonnie, and Clyde. Layla had all of their clothing, favorite toys, and belongings placed inside the houses they were supposed to live in. She wanted them to live on. Scott and everyone else thought it to be creepy and eerie, but they didn't say too much to her about it. Layla wanted what she wanted.

Though there had been some grave and inevitable bumps in the road, things began to look up. The Wests had taken over Delaware with Deuce still missing in action. There was a bounty on his head, and Meyer and Luna were on the hunt. They'd lost a few soldiers during the takeover, but it was worth it. The money coming out of Delaware was more than they'd expected.

Lucky had made a recovery from her assault to some extent, but the beating caused her to look like a stroke victim. She had a droopy eye, some numbness on the right side of her face, and her speech was slurred. Her beauty wasn't what it was before. The doctors proclaimed that she was lucky to be alive. Whenever Lucky saw her reflection, she would cringe with shame and hatred. Her attackers not only left her scarred physically but mentally. She felt ugly. She felt she had let her family down. She could never forget what they did to her in that van that night.

Meyer would try to bring his sister some comfort, telling her how many people he and Luna killed in her honor, but it hurt too much. She was still in the family business, but she felt unwanted, especially by Whistler, who had been ignoring her phone calls and avoiding her.

Initially, Whistler was there for her, taking care of her and trying to nurse her back to health. But Lucky had gotten clingier since being scarred, and she wanted to announce to her family she and Whistler were together. Whistler was against it.

Lucky showed up unannounced at Whistler's apartment one night dressed in her finest outfit. Although she had the droopy eye and wasn't herself completely, she still had a nice figure, and she still had needs. Whistler was the only man she wanted. She marched into the building and proceeded to his apartment door. She knocked loudly.

The knocking and bell ringing stirred Whistler from his sleep. He glanced at the time, and it was three in the morning. He removed himself from the bed, and away from his naked young beauty with long blonde hair and a perfect figure. The pussy was phenomenal.

He put on his designer robe, removed his pistol from the dresser, and walked to the door. Looking through the peephole he saw Lucky standing in his hallway and released an exaggerated sigh. "Fuckin' bitch!" he whispered. He opened the door just a little, preventing her from marching into his place. "You know what time it is, Lucky?"

"I came to see you, Whistler. I missed you," she said.

"Go home, Lucky."

"No. Let me in!" she demanded.

"Go home, Lucky. I'm not in the mood for this."

"Why won't you let me in, Whistler? Huh? You got some bitch in there with you? That's why? Who you fuckin'? Why are you fuckin' avoiding me? Why don't you answer my fuckin' calls?"

Whistler was keeping his cool while Lucky was creating a scene. She was emotional, and emotions were a very dangerous thing, especially in the business they were in.

"Listen, we'll talk later. I promise you. I have some early morning business to attend to, and I need some sleep," he said coolly.

"Don't lie to me, Whistler. Don't play me or I'll tell my father about us," she threatened.

"You know what? We'll tell him together," he said out the blue.

The comment threw her off guard. "What? Are you serious?"

"I am. I can't hide us from him anymore. He needs to know."

It wasn't what she'd expected to hear from him, but it sounded so good. She smiled. Her attitude changed. Her eyes lit up with a smile. "When?"

"Let's meet later this week and come up with a plan on how to tell him about us. Cool?"

She nodded.

"But for now, I need my rest, Lucky. I have a really busy day tomorrow."

She nodded.

Whistler smiled, having calmed down the emotional beast. They kissed in the hallway.

Lucky didn't want to let her man go. He meant everything to her. She believed him. She was nervous, but she figured everything would be okay. She left with a different mood, a more positive feeling.

Whistler closed his door and made a phone call. "Yeah, it's me. We need to talk. I have something for you."

Lucky drove in her expensive Benz Wagon on the Belt Parkway, going from Queens to Brooklyn. It was twilight and a chilly night. She listened to some Alicia Keys and did the speed limit, being in no rush. Trying to get her life back on track was a grueling process. From the therapy to the medication, there were days when she didn't know if she was coming or going. But one thing was for sure—she knew her family had her back. They had the money and the means to secure her with whatever she needed. She was seen by some of the finest doctors in the city, and her recovery treatment was costly, but Scott was doing everything he could for his daughter. But she still had a lot going on.

Listening to the song, "Un-Thinkable (I'm Ready)", she thought about her lover Whistler. The song nearly made her emotional. Lucky always found herself gripped by the lyrics. Alicia Keys was one of her favorite singers. But soon her song was interrupted by the flashing police lights in her rearview mirror. She was being pulled over. Lucky didn't understand why. She wasn't speeding.

"What the fuck!" She steered the Benz off the highway and onto the shoulder.

She sat in the driver's seat, watching the cop's every move in her mirrors, from his marked car to her side door. He tapped on the glass.

Lucky rolled her window down and asked, "What's the problem, officer?"

"License and registration please?"

Lucky had no problem delivering the material into his hands. Her car was legit, her license was clean, and everything was in order. She figured it to be a routine stop. But he still didn't explain the reason for the impulsive traffic stop.

"Why did you pull me over, officer?"

Still, no reply from him. Instead, he got on his police radio and called it in. It didn't take long for another cop to arrive on the scene.

Seeing this was making Lucky nervous now. She didn't understand what was going on. Soon, several officers surrounded her car and were telling her to step out of the car.

"For what? What the fuck did I do?" she barked at them.

"We need to do a search of the vehicle," one said.

"What? Search my car for what?"

"Ma'am, we need for you to step out of the vehicle," he said sternly.

The officers were adamant, but Lucky knew her rights. They had to have a reason.

Their reason was, "We've received a tip that this vehicle is transporting narcotics."

Lucky knew it was bullshit. While angrily removing herself from the Benz, she said, "You'll be hearing from my fuckin' lawyer!"

Immediately, the traffic stop became a dance and show with police dogs on the scene. Lucky stood there in her faux suede belted jacket flabbergasted.

The police and the dogs went through her vehicle and discovered several kilos of cocaine. It was enough narcotics to put her away for life.

Lucky was floored. "That's not mine!" she shouted. "Y'all are setting me up!"

"Ma'am, you're under arrest for possession of a controlled substance," the cop said, pulling out his handcuffs. Then he read her the Miranda rights and handcuffed her.

Lucky wanted to resist. There was no way the drugs found in her vehicle belonged to her. Someone had planted them inside her trunk. But who?

She sulked as she was placed in the back seat of the marked police car. She watched the cops unload five kilos of cocaine from the trunk. There were two reasons she knew someone was out to get her—she didn't move cocaine, and she never rode dirty. They had transporters and mules who did that. She would never put herself at risk. She needed to call her father, and she needed to get in contact with their high-priced attorney, Ross Gadberry. At eight hundred dollars an hour, he was one of the best attorneys in the city to have on retainer.

Lucky didn't feel so lucky. Her life was turning into shit. She sat in the Brooklyn precinct moping while handcuffed to the long, hard bench. It was turning into a long night. She had been waiting to make her one phone call for nearly two hours. Cops and detectives busied themselves with paperwork and arrests, and she wasn't a concern yet. It was like a waiting game.

Her one phone call finally available, she called Gadberry to inform him of her sudden arrest. She knew he could get in touch with her father. He told her to say nothing and that he'd be down to the precinct with her father shortly.

While she was processed into custody, the arresting officer noted that her real name was Lucky Luciana West. He was surprised that her parents would name their daughter Lucky Luciana.

"Lucky Luciana, as in Lucky Luciano?"

"Yes. Is there a problem with my name?"

He chuckled. "It's a unique name for a girl."

"I'm not a girl, I'm a woman."

"Eighteen years old with five kilos in the trunk of your car . . . I guess you're not," the officer replied.

Lucky's droopy eye and her sharp appearance and attitude intrigued the officer. "Funny," he said, "have you ever seen a picture of Lucky Luciano?"

"No. I haven't."

For amusement, he googled the legendary gangster, and Lucky stared at his picture. He had the same droopy eye as her. What were the odds? The officer told her his history. She had never connected it.

"I wasn't born like this," she said. She explained to him she had been brutally beaten, and they'd never caught her attackers. She criticized the NYPD for not doing their jobs when she was beaten, but they had time to arrest and set up innocent people like her.

He chuckled at her story, enraging Lucky. "Don't you think that you and your family are taking this obsession with gangsters too far? You want to be a kingpin like him? Well, you're on your way, sweetheart. Five kilos is nothing to sneeze at."

"The drugs aren't mine!" she exclaimed.

"It's your life."

Lucky frowned.

The cop explained Lucky Luciano's history. He too, had been kidnapped and severely beaten, and left for dead somewhere in Staten Island, but he didn't die, hence the name "Lucky" Luciano. He had been arrested many times, then indicted and sentenced to 30 to 50 years in the state penitentiary.

"You know, your life is somewhat mirroring his," the cop said.

Hearing the similarities left Lucky speechless. She had seen old movies about the gangsters from that era, but she'd never read the true histories about her parents' idols. She felt that her family was in grave danger.

35

Max sat in the prison cafeteria with her cronies eating a stale lunch and half-listening to them converse about frivolous things. Max's attention was fixed on a new inmate across the room. Nadia was doing a few years for check fraud and identity theft, and Max found her the perfect target to help her carry out her revenge against Layla. It had taken some time, but Max had another plan set up. Max couldn't forget or forgive Layla for what she'd done to her and now her friend Shiniquia. Layla thought she could always get away with murder, acting like she ran the world. She had to pay for her sins, and Max was ready to be the Grim Reaper.

Nadia had a boyfriend named Miguel, who Max would have carry out the next half of her plan.

Max got up from her table and went and sat across from Nadia. "You think about my proposal?"

Nadia was hesitating to answer. She had thought about it. Max had status, from the inmates to the guards, so Nadia knew that she was nothing to play with. She wanted no problems inside the prison.

"You and your boyfriend Miguel do this favor for me, and I can guarantee you protection in here," Max said.

Nadia was young, curvy, and cute. The dykes and the butches inside LCIW were ready to have their turn with her. They wanted her badly, enticed by the girl's full lips and long, black hair. The inmates wanted

Nadia to become their baby doll, or personal Barbie Doll. It was easy to tell that Nadia was a scared first-timer. Nadia's fear would become useful for Max. She reminded Max of herself over twenty years ago—pretty, scared, and swallowed up by fear.

"I can protect you in here, Nadia. A favor for a favor," Max said.

"He'll do it," Nadia murmured.

Max was pleased to hear the good news.

Max heard more good news about Lucky's arrest. Max had originally planned to have Lucky set up on a gun charge. Miguel would plant the weapon, call in on the snitch line, and knock Lucky. Max had already arranged for her to be murdered while on Rikers Island awaiting trial. Then it would be on to the next one. Lucky's story would not end like Luciano's.

So imagine the shock and delight when Max heard from Layla that Lucky was knocked for possession of five kilos of that pure white.

Max had been sending her commissary home in a money order to her aging, ailing mother. It totaled ten grand. It was time-consuming, but she was ready to implement her scheme against the West family.

Miguel was ex-military and ex-con. He'd done some time in Attica for a gun charge. His background was shady enough for Max to trust him with murder for hire. He needed the money, and she needed closure.

Max's mother was reluctant to go with her daughter's plan at first, but she eventually left the ten grand in Miguel's mailbox. He had a simple task, and he was determined to pull it off and aid his girlfriend. He knew her life depended on it.

EPILOGUE

2016

Max entered the large room feeling anxious. She was up for parole. She couldn't believe that she would be released if the parole hearing went her way. So much time had passed that she'd forgotten what it felt like to be free and what the outside world looked like. Everything had to have changed dramatically after twenty-two years.

Looking her best in front of the parole committee, her hair styled in a long ponytail, she sat in the folding chair and looked at the several men and women seated a distance from of her. She had to convince these people she was a changed woman.

Max became Maxine in front of the parole committee. She smiled, took a deep breath, and relaxed. They were reviewing her files, and some controversial incidents were on her record. But this was her time to tell her side of the story and to communicate her argument for parole.

Each man and woman stared at Maxine, judging her and trying to read if she was worthy of parole.

"You've done over twenty years in prison. Do you feel that you've been rehabilitated?" one of them asked her.

Did she feel that she'd been rehabilitated? Yes, she'd been transformed all right, becoming a predator inside rather than prey. Prison had changed her in ways she couldn't imagine. She was definitely a different person from twenty-two years earlier. So, yes, she believed that she had been rehabilitated.

"I do, sir."

The committee's job was to know about the parolee—in the interest of public safety—and the needs of the individual inmate. The parole board evaluated the seriousness of Maxine's crime. The fact that she had beaten a pregnant girl to death, killing the baby too, left a bad taste in people's mouths, even twenty-two years later.

Another board member asked, "If released, what are your plans?"

Her plans were about revenge, but she couldn't tell them that.

With a straight face, Maxine looked at them and replied, "I always wanted to become a lawyer. I still feel that dream is attainable for me. But I would have to start over from the beginning—relearn and reevaluate my life. But I'm willing to work hard and make up for so much lost time."

The board wrote notes about her response in their books.

They questioned her about the violence from her time in Bedford Hills to LCIW.

"I came in here young, stupid, scared, and lost. I had no direction, and there were some bad influences in the beginning, but at some point you need to find yourself. I did my time finding myself instead of losing control. I learned to do my time wisely, instead of letting the time do me. I'm ready to restart my life and make a difference somehow. And I'm sorry for what I did. There's not a day that goes by that I don't feel regret and remorse—that I don't think about the lives I destroyed. I was a stupid kid who did some awful things, but that person is long gone."

Maxine sat stiff and firm, not wavering with her answer, but she couldn't tell if she was influencing them or not. There was no need for her to become unhinged in front of the parole board. Either they would grant her freedom or not. Ironically, she had gotten so used to the prison life that freedom seemed far-fetched.

To Max's shock, she was granted parole. The Louisiana prison system was becoming too crowded, so the state was giving first-time offenders parole. She would be released after twenty-two years behind bars. Now, she could execute her sweet revenge up close and personally.

THAT WAS ONLY
THE BEGINNING

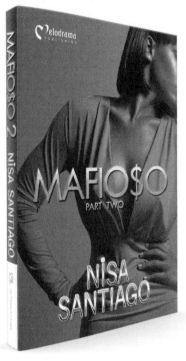

BLAST FROM THE PAST

Payback is a bitch named Maxine. She's a once-demure law student who's finally free after serving time for a murder she didn't commit. Maxine has a score to settle, and she's now driven to return the favor of destruction. Her kill list, unknowingly financed by her frenemy, Layla, is steadily shrinking with bodies dropping all over NYC.

Scott and Layla West have buried their children one-by-one from what appears to be random accidents. With the top Mafioso distracted by grief and territory battles, a traitor has infiltrated the tight-knit organization. Scott and Layla's misfortunes only multiply when they realize they've been targeted all along.

THE SERIES BY

EXCERPT FROM
MAFIOSO - PART TWO

Y 'all actually believe that Gotti, Bonnie, and Clyde were killed over a drug beef by a street thug named Deuce? A man who months ago, had no idea we existed?" Whistler argued.

"It's gotta be him. Who else has means and motive to touch one of our own?" Bugsy asked.

"This is the handiwork of someone who's smart but also has patience. A hood nigga like Deuce would have tried to take out the head and watch the body fall. He woulda come at Scott, not his kids. These hits were professional. No witnesses, no fuckin' warning!"

"You talkin' 'bout some mastermind—some character out a fuckin' novel," Meyer cursed.

"I'm saying to everyone in this room that these aren't business-related murders. It feels personal and deliberate. They were methodical and well planned."

"Then give us a name, Whistler," Bugsy said.

"He don't have a fuckin' name. He's full of shit," Meyer said. "Makin' shit bigger than what it is. This is a drug beef, niggas. We fightin' over territory block by block. You know what it is."

Whistler's face tightened like a rubber band stretching to its limits. He clenched his fists and was three seconds from leaping over the table at Meyer. The boy was a hothead with no common sense. If it weren't for Scott, Meyer would have been dog food on the streets.

The brothers continued to bicker back and forth with Whistler, who always felt he was the smartest guy in the room. Whistler had no name for the assailants, but he knew it wasn't Deuce's doing. He needed to investigate more. There was someone in the shadows coming at them. Their true enemy had not yet revealed himself. Deuce executing this shit just wasn't feasible. Whistler needed to make Scott and Layla believe that. But, they were too emotional. They were angry and wanted bloodshed. Someone needed to die, which was understandable.

"Give me time, and I'll find a name. I'll locate the muthafuckas responsible for these attacks," Whistler assured Scott. "I'll burn them alive for ever fuckin' with the West Empire."

BUT WAIT!
THERE'S MORE

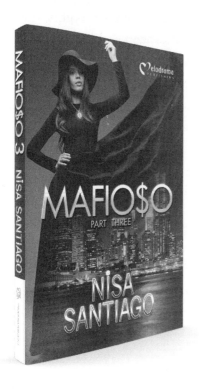

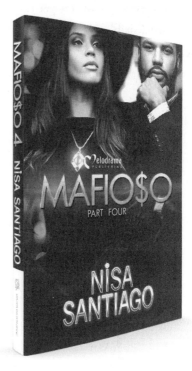

THE SERIES BY
NISA
SANTIAGO

IT'S ABOUT TO GET DIRTY

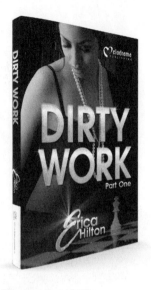 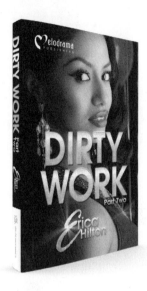

Poisoned Pawn

Harlem brothers, Kip and Kid Kane, are like night and day. While Kip is with his stick-up crew hitting ballers and shot-callers, the wheelchair-bound Kid is busy winning chess tournaments and being a genius.

Kip's ex, Eshon, and her girls, Jessica and Brandy, put in work for Kip's crew as the E and J Brandy bitches. Eshon wants Kip, but Kip is always focused on the next heist—the next big come-up.

When given an assignment by the quirky Egyptian kingpin, Maserati Meek, Kip jumps at the chance to level up to bigger scores. While doing Maserati Meek's Dirty Work, Kip and his crew find that doing business with crazy pays handsomely. But at what cost? Insanity leads to widespread warfare, and the last man standing will have to take down the warlord.

Tired of Being Broke?
Join the *Club*!

Ever wonder why it seems like the cheap girls of the world belong to an exclusive club? Wonder why they have a Zen-like nature while you're struggling to make the rent? Answer: Money.

It's high time to save more and stress less. Step up and accept the challenge. Initiate yourself into the Cheap Girls Club.

Most wealthy people are cheap and know there's more than one way to be charitable. In this how-to manual for financial fierceness, Winslow explains how she found value in being six-figures in debt. Through honest, inspiring stories she spills the tea on what she did to get on the right path to financial freedom.

Learn the secrets of how the wealthy look at money differently. Learn to be Cheap! #CheapGirlsClubChallenge

KNOCK, KNOCK.

 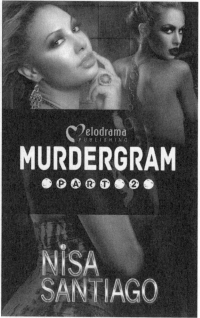

THE EPIC SERIES BY

NISA SANTIAGO

LET'S BUILD.

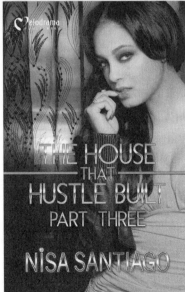

A Series by
Nisa Santiago

Don't Let the Dollface Fool You

 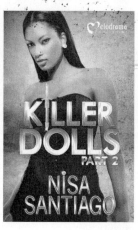 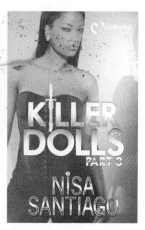

NOW AVAILABLE EVERYWHERE